THROWN

AWAY

BOOK 1

IN A FALLEN WORLD

GLYNN JAMES

IN A FALLEN WORLD

He sensed them in the darkness, all around, moving quickly through the building, room by room as they searched. Every few minutes the silence was broken by loud crashing sounds as they broke into another area, the clatter of broken wood scattering across rotten floorboards and cracked concrete, or the terrible, grief-stricken and desperate cries of those who had been found, their hiding places uncovered. He could hear the thud of boots sometimes, echoing through the corridors, or the creaking of the building's very structure as it protested against the abuse.

Centuries old and given to spontaneous collapse, the tenement buildings of the outer zone had ceased to be safe long before any of their current residents had been born, but the crumbling ruins were the only real shelter for many of the inhabitants of the zone, the only place to hide from the danger on the streets or the often unforgiving weather.

Most of the dangers lay outside of the crumbling walls – things that wandered the streets at night that were far from human, but the hunting squads from the city travelled deep into the darkness of the buildings, seeking those who would avoid capture. Finally, the noise that everyone dreaded could be heard in the distance – the rising hum and the sharp crackling buzz as a stun rifle was fired.

Jack sat in silence, listening, willing his nerves to calm and his heart rate to slow. The sounds were getting closer now, and he knew they were in a nearby corridor, possibly just a few rooms away. He heard boots shuffling along the floor, and the crash of rubbish as it was kicked aside – the barrier that he had built outside provided no protection, was merely an inconvenience for the heavily armoured troopers whose faces had never been seen, at least by anyone who remained to tell of them.

Jack had never known where the raiding parties took the captured, for no one ever returned. There were always tales and rumours of course, but no one that he had ever met had confirmed any of them.

The corridors of the sprawling, old building were littered with the junk and debris of decades, most of it useless and left there because there was nowhere else for it to go. But the trash also acted as a territorial marker, a sign of neighbouring borders, of marked out claims. Often it was piled up to waist height, to act as a makeshift defensive barrier, and a way to slow intruders down or ward them away. Folks who lived in the area would know to stay away, and recognise the barrier for what it was, but the Hunters saw it as a sign of life, of someone to capture and drag away to their prison vehicles. The vehicles had no windows on the sides or the back, and Jack suspected it might be completely dark inside them, but that was something else that no one had confirmed. No one ever came back.

His heart thumped harder in his chest and he doubled his efforts to control his breathing, to remain silent, but a cold trickle of sweat heightened the twitching of already ragged nerves as it ran down his neck. Jack knew there was a chance, if only very small, that they could pass him by. The Hunters might enter the room, their pinpoint searchlights flickering over the walls, passing over the cracked paint and the curled and mould-ridden wallpaper, skittering over the rubble and litter covered ground and not stopping as they zipped past the broken wardrobe that was his hiding place. Even if they did look into the wardrobe, they could still miss him as he lay huddled in the bottom, covered by rags and old clothing. With this thought, he crouched lower and did his best to *be* a pile of discarded junk.

It was possible. *But maybe this is my time?* he thought. *They could pass you by, like before, but they are smart, not stupid, and you know that they see more than you think they do, don't you? What if they did take you?*

5

He tried to ignore the thoughts. From his hiding place he could only see a tiny slice of the derelict room beyond. Both doors of the wardrobe were still attached, even if they did hang at odd angles, and he had pulled them as closed as they would go. It only left a few inches in between the doors, so his vision was limited, but his hearing was sharp, and when the first Hunter stepped into the room Jack slowed his breathing to almost nothing. Instinct kicked in and he lay there, perfectly still and silent, not knowing how long he could keep it up, but hoping that the search would be over quickly.

Slow and shallow, slow and shallow, he thought. Repeating the mantra in his mind, over and over. If he could just keep this up long enough, and if he made no noise, they would go away, wouldn't they? The old man that Jack had once travelled with, so very long ago, had taught him how to hold his breath and stay perfectly still, had even beaten him with a stick until he got it right. And so, over the years, he had done this before in many other places and not been found.

But I've also never been this close to them, he thought. Not this close. *Just a few feet away. They can see through walls – that's what some folks claimed, and they can see you in the darkness.* His breathing wavered very slightly at this thought. If they could see him anyway, wasn't he just delaying the inevitable, waiting and waiting only to be taken like all the others? But what choice did he have?

The same choice you had back then, he thought. *You have your machetes. But what good would they be against the armour of the Hunters? If you had the guts to use them, you would have done it back then, back when it really mattered.*

The Hunters never searched thoroughly, they just swept through an area like a hurricane, raiding entire buildings in just minutes, satisfied if they found someone to stun and carry away. Jack would hear the buzz of a stun rifle and the thud as a discovered victim hit the ground, and then heavy boots clomping away as the Hunters carried their latest catch to the vehicles that awaited them in the street – the vehicles with no windows.

Sometimes there would be a struggle if the Hunters found a group of people together, but the fight was always over quickly. There was little defence against the weapons that the soldiers used. Sticks, knives and metal pipes were no match for reactive armour and a stun rifle that could knock you out cold at fifty yards, with one shot. Fists were useless against a shock-stick that could render you unconscious with just one strike, twitching and writhing on the ground as the electrical pulse surged through your nervous system. And if the resistance was too high then they would just throw in a grenade and stun everyone in the room. One loud *thump* and it would be over. Except the grenades didn't always stun – sometimes they caused more damage than that. Sometimes there would be bodies left behind.

The outer zone of the city – the area beyond the glowing barrier – was massive. Thousands and thousands of square miles of ruined, crumbling decay. Endless desolate streets lined with empty shells that had once been buildings – their windows shattered, doors long taken for firewood, bricks and stone cracked and collapsing, leaving holes that looked like gaping wounds. It was among these ruins that the destitute – the people not allowed to live on the inside of the barrier – were forced to make their homes, to scavenge and scrape some form of life from the remains of a fallen world. These people were never permitted within the confines of the barrier, but for some reason that no one had ever discovered, the people on the inside were capturing the ones on the outside, and in large numbers.

Where were they taken? This was the question everyone wanted an answer to, but one that was never given. There were places that were left alone – larger outer zone communities, workhouses – anywhere that had a dense population – these weren't raided. Maybe there was too much risk involved attacking such heavily defended locations? He didn't know. What he did know was that to claim your own pitch in many of the bigger hovels was a fight that most people couldn't win, so they were forced to live in the surrounding ruins. Those were the ones who would be hunted and taken.

It had been nearly three months since Jack was last in an area targeted by the Hunters. With such a vast city to search, it was rare to even see them in the distance. They only came down from the inner city once every few weeks, that much he did know. But knowing where and when they would strike next was an art form that very few had mastered, a total mystery to most.

And it was so fast when it happened, the huge Dropship soaring across the sky at a speed that was dazzling for such a massive behemoth of a vehicle. It would land within seconds of appearing on the horizon, the huge black shape plummeting towards the ground as if it were about to crash. But it never did crash. Seconds after the blast of jets were unleashed, the Dropship was on the ground, spewing out a torrent of fast-moving armoured carrier vehicles that burst through the clouds of dust kicked up by the beast's arrival. The vehicles quickly sped through the streets at a terrifying speed, and when they arrived at their target location, dozens of armed squads would jump from the trucks, surging into the ruined buildings in search of vagrants. In search of prey.

Jack tried to recall the first time that he had seen a raid, and the picture came to him almost immediately, blanking out the sounds of the Hunters moving in the darkness around him. There were several of them in the room now, scanning, searching, but even with capture in such close proximity, his mind still drifted away, seeking a place to escape to.

JUST ONCE

Many years before...

How old had he been at the time? He had been very young, seven years old at most, and life in the ruins was still a thing of terror for him – a time spent hiding in dark corners and shadows, avoiding the folks that searched the ruins. It was a time of catching rats or mice and scratching for life, even though it was one spent in near constant starvation. That he had survived those days was a miracle in itself, for many others that he had known hadn't. He tried to wipe their faces from his mind and think back to the one scene that might ease him.

So many of them lost, he thought. *So many friends, and some not so friendly.* It didn't matter which, though. They were all gone, now. Taken was taken and dead was still dead, unless you were one of the things that roamed the streets at night, and no one really knew much about why they were still there.

The building Jack had been hiding in the first time he'd experienced a Hunter raid, all those years ago, wasn't in the block that the soldiers had targeted.

11

Lucky, that's what you were. Others hadn't been as lucky as you.

He remembered hiding for a while, curled up in the corner of a bathroom, high up in the crumbling shell of an abandoned apartment building. He had been tired, almost completely exhausted, and had huddled inside the recess behind the cracked sink to sleep for a while. He'd found the spot a few days before, as he entered the bathroom in search of water. Some of the pipes and taps in the old buildings still gave occasional bursts of fresh water. No one knew how or why, but the old man that taught Jack how to slow-breathe also said that some of it came from hidden water springs deep under the ground, and that it would occasionally overflow into the old water systems.

The hole behind the sink was almost unnoticeable even from a few feet away, and Jack certainly hadn't spotted it immediately, and probably never would have, had he not also been searching for metal to trade as well as water. A scavenger group living not far away loved their metals, and plumbing pipes were still the most abundant source, if you knew where to find them. As he had crawled behind the sink to see if any of the original piping was still there, he found that the area opened up into a small compartment just big enough for him, and a little left over to stretch his legs if need be.

Hiding places such as that would serve him for many years.

That first experience of the noise of the incoming Dropship was the most terrifying. The roar was louder than anything he had ever heard, and since he was unable to see its source, it sounded like some huge beast was about to trample the whole city. But the noise stopped in an instant, and the sound of smaller engines cut through the quiet. Jack had crawled from his hiding place, curiosity overcoming his fear, and peeped out of the broken window just above the sink.

The streets were buzzing with large grey trucks, and he could see soldiers dressed in grey armour rushing into the buildings nearby. They carried weapons that he had never seen before – large black rifles that looked heavy and awkward, and long black sticks with tips that glowed blue in the darkness.

He watched, struck motionless with fascination, as a group of people in a building just two blocks away were roughly ushered into the back of one of the vehicles, and a surge of fear hit him. What if they came to his building? Still, he watched from the window as the vehicles came and went, and once he realised that they weren't coming into his building, he tentatively crept closer to the window and watched. He still kept to the shadows, fearing that one glimpse of a person in a neighbouring building would set the hounds upon him and the few vagrants that lived in the lower levels, but he couldn't help but watch. Some morbid fascination kept his eyes glued to the chaos just yards away as more soldiers piled from the backs of vehicles and ran into the surrounding buildings.

Heavy boots kicked down doors, and long black sticks smashed through windows. Minutes later they reappeared, dragging the unlucky people that they had found, throwing them into the back of their trucks. This went on for ten minutes or so, until finally a group of four soldiers approached the front of a dilapidated and crumbling storefront opposite the tenement building he was hiding in.

Then the real chaos started.

The old store was where the gang of Scavs – scavengers – had been holed up, and Jack estimated there had to be at least thirty of them in there. They were inoffensive folk, if a little rough, but they left him alone, never harassing him or any of the other dwellers in the area. It wasn't their way. They weren't territorial, and would be gone in a few months, maybe even weeks – that was how the Scav clans worked. Jack had met their kind before on the few occasions when he ended up near the outer circle – the furthest parts of the city from the centre. It was usually where their kind lived. Except they moved around a lot, never staying in one place for more than a few weeks, scouring the area for metals to salvage and then moving on.

But he had no idea just how heavily armed Scav clans could be until the moment the four Hunters headed for the front door of the store.

The streets were silent, except for the distant crashes of doors being broken, and the cries of the discovered. Most of the search was over and many of the trucks were already filled with those unfortunate enough to have been found. When the four soldiers got to the door of the store, and the first lifted his foot to smash a way in, the doors burst open, both swinging wide. The first Hunter, one boot lifted in the air and now off-balance, fell backwards, struck down by the force of the door, and that was what saved him from dying with the other three. Even as they started to raise their stun rifles, a deluge of weapon-fire erupted from within the building. Jack had never heard such a tremendous and destructive noise. Flashes of blue light rocketed out of the double doors and tore into the three soldiers. All three fell to the ground, their bodies torn apart.

The Scavs weren't using weapons that just stunned.

The fourth Hunter rolled to the side of the doors, jumped up and started to run from the store, but then the Scavs were flooding out of the front doors, most of them carrying bags and sacks as they turned and ran, but the first half a dozen were armed with heavy, black weapons. The fourth Hunter got maybe twenty yards before they gunned him down in the middle of the street, flashes of blue energy thundering into him, tearing the limbs from his body.

In the distance, a klaxon sounded – an alarm from the direction of the Dropship, and Jack crouched down, further into the darkness, watching as more armoured vehicles sped through the streets, heading in his direction. He looked down at the store below, and saw the last of the Scavs grabbing the Hunters' rifles and pulling belts and other equipment from the dead bodies before they ran, moving swiftly into the darkness of the surrounding streets.

By the time the half-dozen armoured trucks arrived, the Scavs were long gone and all that was left were the four dead, stripped bodies.

It was the only time Jack had ever seen or heard of someone putting up a fight and winning.

HUNTED

Now, sitting in the wardrobe, pretending to be a pile of rags and holding his breath, he wished he had one of those weapons, in case the Hunters, just feet away, managed to detect him, and that he'd had one of those Scav guns a few years ago.

Then it never would have happened...

...and there it was, again. The ever-haunting memory he wished he could remove. But frustration had once again brought the memory rushing back, his brain desperate for distraction.

Jack had been furious at the boy for drawing in his magazine, so angry that he had stood there, towering over the child, shouting angrily at him. Until he saw how small the boy was, the tiny figure looking at the floor, his rounded face bright red with the shame of what he had done. They were Jack's things. His magazines. His way to learn about the past. The boy had known that and should have known better than to de-face one of them. Jack had been so angry with him that he hadn't heard the Dropship approaching until they barely had the time to react — so little time to hide.

On that day, because of his scolding, the boy looked

as fragile as he had the day they'd met.

THEY TOOK HIS SHOES

Three years before...

The boy had been sitting at the side of the road the day that Jack met him. The child's scrawny arms were wrapped around his knees, his head bent low as he shivered. It wasn't too cold, but then the child wasn't wearing the extra layers that Jack was. Where Jack had two shirts underneath his heavy leather coat, and black overall bottoms pulled over his jeans, the boy was dressed in a torn and filthy t-shirt and a pair of thin, ripped trousers.

You saw *things* almost every day in the outer zone — people in doorways, huddled against the weather, their eyes dark and tired, their faces gaunt, but you just moved on. Life was harsh and deadly, and to even attempt to help others was considered a foolish way to shorten your own life.

Jack had just been to The Crossing, a walled and defended section of the ruins that had grown over many years into a dangerous but necessary marketplace. It was a hovel — one of the small towns that the Hunters ignored. There were many such places dotted around the outer city, thriving hubs of activity where people had gathered and built defences against the world outside, ramshackle shanty towns filled with all manner of folks trying to survive and not wanting to live on the streets of the dead city. But to hold on to a place in one of the towns you had to have resources or weapons, something to ensure that you could keep your pitch. The Crossing was a place that Jack visited regularly, the centre of everything for miles around. That also meant that it was the hang out for every thug, gang or would-be overlord in the area.

But it was also a place to trade. If Jack found something while scavenging, something that had a value to someone, then it was to The Crossing that he would usually take it. Metals, ammunition, paper, plastics, food – anything that could be traded – was wanted by someone there.

He was trudging along the highway, on his way out after trading some lead sheeting he had found in an old factory for a dozen packets of dried biscuits and a bottle of oil, and he had only made it a few hundred yards out of the gates when he crossed another intersection and saw the boy.

Anyone with any sense of self-preservation got off the road, hid away in a building, or just kept moving. The roads going into The Crossing were a place to get yourself killed in a second if you hung around too long. In the shadows of the buildings that lined the street, prospective scavengers lay in wait, watching from their hiding places, just for the moment where someone passed by or stayed too long. Jack had seen many a body in the gutters, stripped of all belongings, throats slit, skin turning pale.

And yet here was this small figure, sitting on the edge of the sidewalk, rocking backwards and forwards.

Jack slowed as he approached and glanced at the gaping hole in the side of the nearest building. It could be a trap, he knew — the child sent outside as bait to draw in some unfortunate victim looking for an easy take, or a fool thinking of offering help. But there was no movement from inside the crumbling building, no eyes watching from the corners, no shadows shifting.

Still, he gripped the handles of his two machetes tightly as he started making his way around the swaying figure, keeping his distance and moving quickly. Yet every few steps he couldn't help but glance at the child — his thin arms, the dirt that covered every inch of him, his body heaving as he sobbed. These were good tricks for a baiter. But then, as Jack started to move away to leave the boy behind and move on, he noticed that the child had nothing on his feet, and that they were bloodied.

The hairs on the back of Jack's neck started to tingle. Why was he stopping? Why did he find himself standing, turning to face the small figure, and taking a step towards him? It made no sense. Even if he hadn't seen watchers in the building, that didn't mean they weren't there.

Right now, there could be a dozen of them creeping around, surrounding him, and preparing to rush in for the kill. He could stand his ground against one, two, maybe even three, but a large gang – the kind of gang that employed baiter tactics to catch foolish, weak-hearted folks that might stop to offer help – no, he wouldn't be able to fight that off.

But there he was, still moving closer. Then he was just a few feet away, looking down at the huddled figure that still hadn't sensed his presence.

"Why are you sitting here?" Jack asked him but was rewarded with no answer. The boy just sat there, rocking and murmuring. Yes, Jack could hear the murmuring now... or was it singing? He listened, peering at the child through narrowed eyes, straining to understand. Didn't he recognise the words from somewhere?

Five green bottles sitting on the wall...

Some sort of saying, or a poem.

One green bottle, should accidentally fall…

The tune was familiar, vague, but familiar. Something from Jack's childhood that he didn't want to remember, but he found that he did.

We used to sing it in nursery school, he thought. The recollection was there, even after all these years, but not clear enough for him to picture it.

And he didn't want to hear it any longer.

"Boy!" he snapped, and the small figure jumped at that, almost falling back as he fumbled to steady himself. The child stared up at Jack, eyes wide and full of terror, his tightly closed lips trembling. At the sight of his fear, Jack's irritation with the song vanished, and he spoke again, more softly.

"What are you doing in the middle of the street?"

The boy looked at him, eyes still wide, and tried to speak, but for a moment nothing seemed to come out but a quiet squeak.

"They took my shoes," the boy finally said, grasping his bloodied feet with pale hands, his eyes bright with tears.

Jack wanted to ask if the boy was a baiter, but knew it was a pointless question. If the child was bait for a gang's trap, it was already too late. Jack would already be caught in it. But there was still no movement in the buildings surrounding them, and no noise but the howl of the wind and a repetitive squeaking noise. A few feet away a rotten sign hung over a door that would once have been the entrance to a shop. The wind blew it backwards and forwards with the same rhythmic motion as the boy's, as he had rocked backwards and forwards just a few moments before. The screech of the plastic, rubbing on the pole that jutted out of the broken brickwork, was long and drawn out, a noise that grated at Jack's nerves.

The boy was still staring at him, his expression weary. He had dark bags under blood-shot eyes, a stark contrast to his pale skin. The boy looked severely malnourished and quite sickly, and those eyes spoke of many nights of missed sleep.

"They took my shoes," the boy repeated.

That was three years ago, he thought.

HUNTED

The Hunters were so close now that Jack thought he could hear their breathing. Pinpoint spotlights continued to flicker across the room, tracing the corners, the places of darkness, the door opposite, and then the window. The thud of boots on the floorboards. He thought for one moment that he heard talking, muffled and low. The soldiers wore helmets that covered their faces completely, and even at security stations near the inner city he had never heard one of them speak or seen their faces. Their armour and helmets made them look like robots, almost inhuman. Whatever conversations they were having must have been via radio, and private, only among themselves.

Through the narrow slit that was his only view of the room, Jack saw the dark shape move, slowly sweeping the area and peering through the two openings that led into the other two rooms in his small, rubbish-littered hideout.

He knew that these places had once been called apartments, and he guessed that centuries ago they would have been homes for people, couples, or even whole families. This much he had learnt from the remnants of magazines and books that could occasionally be found among the ruins and from the signs that he had seen on the stairwells of many of the old buildings. If you took the time to look around, evidence of the old days – from before the time that the world collapsed into the chaos that he'd seen for most his life – was everywhere. Tatty old posters, half worn away by the weather, still clung to the walls, depicting people in some of the strangest clothing he had ever seen – bright and sparkling costumes that surely couldn't have been everyday wear.

Books lying in tattered heaps in the corners of old buildings were also a treasure of tales of the old world. Most of them had been burned for fuel, but occasionally he would come across them, sometimes hidden away where someone hadn't looked. And the magazines and old newspapers – he loved them the most – not only could he learn about things from the long gone, but there were pictures that showed him what things had looked like back then.

Once, in a run-down office building many miles across the city, out near the Ashlands, he had found an article about the very street that he was on. Some sort of horrible act had been committed. A murder, he thought, but it wasn't the scene of uniformed soldiers that had interested him. It had been the buildings in the background of the picture. He could clearly see the very building that he was in, and next to it the vast thing that had once been called The Grand Theatre. Jack didn't know what one of those was, but by the size of the place, he thought it must have been something important.

Two huge towers rose on either side of the main entrance, and a massive board with bright white lettering stood as a bold centrepiece. There were hundreds of people queuing outside the entrance, just yards from a cordoned off area patrolled by men in uniforms. All of those people were waiting to be allowed admittance into the vast building that he knew was now, centuries later, just an empty shell.

Jack had been in there before he discovered the offices nearby, and wondered in awe what the huge room, with the cracked and weathered carpets, was for. In the magazine there was a picture of the interior, with rows upon rows of seats, all filled with smiling people as they waited for whatever spectacle happened at The Grand Theatre. He had presumed that it was some kind of meeting place, and that the stage at one end of the room – now just a hollow hole in the ground with a twisted set of metal stairs leading up to nothing – was where someone important would stand.

So much was hidden away, waiting to be found by

those with an eye for searching. So much still left behind but unnoticed. A keen eye could spot the clues that many had missed, and Jack had collected a few almost intact magazines over the years – something considered valuable just for the paper. And as he sat in the wardrobe, watching the figure of the Hunter move through the room, his gaze stopped on the small pile of magazines across the room in the corner, where he had left them, and when one of the tracer lights passed over them, stopped and went back to settle on the top magazine, his heart started to thump harder.

Stupid.

He had left them out in full view, an obvious sign of at least recent occupancy.

The dark shape of the Hunter moved across the room, rifle sweeping backwards and forwards, covering the door, the windows, and the dark recesses as the soldier approached the corner. The figure moved out of Jack's slice of vision, but he could hear the rustle of paper, pages being flicked through, being disturbed. And then the sound of the same boots again, thudding across the boards, the shadow moving swiftly out of the room and then heading away. They were leaving, treading heavily on creaking floorboards as they moved off down the corridor.

Jack breathed again, still keeping as quiet as he

could, but his lungs had been close to forcing the breath out of him, screaming to inhale more air, and it was a relief to exhale and fill them again. Stupid, he thought. Part-way through the raid he had stopped regulating his breathing and held it. And he'd held it so long that it was too late to exhale without making a loud noise. If the soldiers had been there for a minute longer he wouldn't have been able to keep his breath in, and right now he'd be in the back of their vehicle, on his way to wherever they went.

The urge to look out was almost overwhelming. He needed to see if they had taken his magazines. They were his most prized belongings, picked up here and there from various hidden treasure troves across the city — at least a dozen of them, including the one that the boy had left behind. The one the boy had drawn pictures in.

Now Jack felt the ache in his chest, a pain that he had tried to keep at bay for two years, but sometimes it crept over him at the most unexpected moments. He couldn't think of that right now, mustn't drift back into self-loathing and thoughts of the past that was lost.

He just stayed there, still, impatience burning in his guts, the urge to burst from his hiding place and scramble across the room almost unbearable, knowing that any noise could bring the soldiers back. He cursed his own foolishness. Why had he not just put them in his rucksack? That was where he normally kept them. He had taken them out to look at, and to add his newest finds to the leather sleeve that he kept them in to protect them from damage. Three new magazines to add, and yet he hadn't put them away afterwards. Instead he had drifted off to sleep, leaving them in a pile, and only waking at the tremendous noise of the approaching Dropship. In his panic to hide he had forgotten about the magazines and had just run for the wardrobe.

Now he couldn't see if they were still there, and couldn't see if the Hunter had taken any of them. The paper was worth money to the right buyer, but not as much as their sentimental value to Jack, and nowhere near as much as that magazine with the boy's drawings.

There was no price on that one. Could never be. He had scolded the boy, told him off for defacing what was precious to him, and yet, now, the one with the drawings in it was the most valuable thing to him.

THE RIGHT CHOICE

Three years before...

The boy had no shoes on the day Jack met him, and kept repeating that fact as Jack stood there, considering what to do next.

This isn't my problem, he thought. This is just stupid of me, staying here in full view for too long. I'm an open target. I need to move on.

But what about the child?

I could help him if I chose to, if I was willing to take the burden. Or maybe I could at least take him to The Crossing, and find someone who would want a boy to work for them.

There was no one who could be trusted. Jack sighed. Finally, he decided to just walk away. This was a problem that he didn't need. But then a memory from his own childhood came to him, because Jack had lived on the inside of the barrier once, so very long ago.

ONLY TWO TICKETS

Many years before...

Jack could only have been six or seven years old – he couldn't recall exactly – and all of his memories of those days were remembered like a small child would remember them. He was very young when he stopped living on the inside of the barrier and found himself walking in a line, following other children. He wore no shoes and they were walking over the hard, gravelled ground, out of the security gates and into the crumbling ruins that were the *outside*.

The day before he had been at home, in the warmth, playing with his toys and reading his books. His parents had been packing up everything in the house, or at least most of it. He had peered into his parent's bedroom and saw his mother putting things into a large plastic container that looked like an over-sized suitcase. It wasn't one of their normal suitcases, the purple ones under their bed. This was different. His mother was putting things into it, and then taking them out, and he thought that she seemed to be choosing what to take with her.

They had gone on what his father called vacations, sometimes. It meant leaving, and it meant travelling on the sub-train for a long time, and then arriving at a place where there was sand and lots of water. They would stay there for a few days and then go home again. But this time had been different. All the furniture was covered with plastic sheeting, and the cupboards — which were normally filled with food — were now empty.

He'd gone back to his toys, not paying attention, preferring to use his crayons to draw stick-men with guns shooting monsters, or huge dinosaurs eating helpless victims. But then he heard raised voices from his parents' room. They were arguing, he'd thought. It wasn't a frequent thing. His parents were both quiet people, prone to long periods of silence. He couldn't hear what the argument was about, but vividly recalled one phrase that his mother said.

"But there are only two tickets."

Those were the only words of the conversation that he'd caught, and it was the last thing he ever heard his mother say. A short while later he heard the front door open, and then shut, and then two men were in the room with him, ushering him out of the house.

Jack knew now that his parents had made some kind of decision that day, all those years ago, and the choice meant that he would go somewhere else. He'd figured that much out for himself. There were only two tickets to whatever journey his parents had gone on, and therefore, he couldn't go with them. Forty years must have passed, and he still didn't know where they'd gone. He'd always thought that you came back from a vacation.

As he'd walked in line with the other children, fear building in his chest as he saw the massive walls that protected the inner city – which had been his home for the entirety of his life – becoming more distant, further behind them with every step that they took out into the ruins. He remembered that his feet hurt on the gravel, and they bled, just like the feet of the boy as he sat at the side of the road that day.

A choice had been made a very long time ago that led to Jack walking barefoot away from every comfort he'd ever known, into a life much more precarious, harsh, and dangerous.

LET'S GET MOVING

Two years before...

Why had he made a decision, right then, to not leave the boy without first offering to help? Had he seen something of himself there, sitting on the side of the road? Had he seen that the boy was like him?

"Come on," Jack said, looking around, scoping the streets and the abandoned buildings for movement. If the boy had been bait, the attack would already have been upon him.

But that didn't mean they were safe.

Jack started to walk along the sidewalk, his machetes still drawn, eyes flickering over every possible hiding place. But when he stopped at the intersection and glanced back, the boy hadn't followed him. The child was standing, but not walking. He was just standing there, his tiny, round face screwed up with indecision.

The kid is terrified, he thought, *and can't trust me*. He couldn't blame the child for being cautious or afraid, but alive was always better than dead, and if the boy stayed where he was, he would be dead before morning. Maybe the kid didn't realise that?

He sighed, impatient but reluctant to leave the boy to his fate.

"I've got food," Jack shouted. "And… we'll try to find something for your feet."

The boy's expression changed at that, a flicker of hope removing the wide-eyed fear from his eyes.

"New shoes?" the boy asked as he took a single, tentative step forward.

"Yes!" Jack said, already beginning to regret what this offer would cost him. "But let's get moving." He waved his arm, indicating the buildings around them. "You think losing your shoes is bad? There are worse things that folks will do to you if you stay here too long."

Jack headed off down the street, deciding if the boy followed him he would help him, at least for a while. But if he didn't follow, then it was his choice, his life. Jack was already putting himself out, he thought. If the boy didn't come, then fate would decide what would happen to him.

But the boy did follow, and was soon jogging along beside him, not complaining even once. If his feet hurt him as they travelled away from The Crossing, the child didn't make it apparent.

36

Jack's hideout at the time was a long walk away, at least four miles from The Crossing, and he didn't stop to rest. It would be dark in a few hours and he wanted to be barricaded in by then, hidden away from what prowled the streets at night.

As they walked, he glanced over at the boy, realising for the first time just how small the child was. He couldn't have been older than six, about the age that Jack had been when he had escaped from the workhouse.

THE WORKHOUSE

Many years before...

Even considering all the difficulties of life on the outside, among the ruins of the outer zone with the dangerous things that haunted that skeletal landscape and the gangs of vicious and cold-hearted folk that prowled and picked at the debris for anything edible or salvageable, Jack's short time in the workhouse near the border had been worse.

After the long walk through the ruins, following the other kids in the chain gang led by a dozen armed and rough-looking men, they had arrived at what would be his home for six months.

It was a sprawl of several buildings, most of them crumbling and dangerously unstable, housing over a hundred kids and their captors. For Jack, the place was a shock beyond anything he had experienced in his short life. There was little care taken for those that were held captive and made to work in the derelict warehouse and machine facility, barely a mile from the pulsing barrier that protected the wealthy and the fortunate. Most days were spent working on huge machines, the purpose of which Jack had never really known, and most nights were spent on the cold, hard ground, trying to sleep through nightmares and wondering when the next meal would come.

Jack remembered spending hours upon hours shovelling dirty, black rocks called *coal,* from the mountainous piles that the delivery ships would dump on the open grounds outside the main building, into rickety wheelbarrows that were then rushed away by other children. There were no adults working the dumping ground. A few sat around the outside fence, their arms folded, watching intently for a child that wasn't working as hard as the rest.

He remembered aching constantly from the strain of the work. The small muscles of a child were never meant to haul the loads that they were forced to manage every day for almost the entire time that the sun was in the sky. And on top of the muscle-draining work of lifting shovel after shovel, there was the panicked and rushed moment when a new Dropship would arrive and no one on the ground knew where it was going to dump its next delivery load. For a frantic couple of minutes, the hundred or so children in the yard would stand and watch the sky, waiting as the ship slowed to a halt. And when it released its load, those underneath would run as fast as they could.

Why had it been that way? he wondered, as he always did when memories of the workhouse came back to him. Surely the guards could have called the kids away from the open area while the ship had delivered the next mountain of coal? Surely it would have made much more sense to do that? Then there wouldn't have been the accidents. People could be cold and uncaring in the outer district, and many were cruel, but none as bad as the men who made the yard-workers stay out in the open when the coal was delivered.

He had seen them, the guards, making bets, and had heard names mentioned, though fortunately never his own. Who would be the next to go? – had been the subject of the money exchanged. Who would be the next child killed by falling coal?

The day that he escaped, along with many others, had been one of the times that someone had died under the avalanche of the black rocks. Except on that day it hadn't been a child that was killed, but one of the guards. No one planned for it to work out how it had, and he thought that not a single kid in the yard had expected the ship to drop early, and so close to the edge of the yard. Maybe it had been a mistake by the pilot, or the crew in the cargo chamber of the ship. Someone could have pulled the lever before they were supposed to and *whoosh*, away went the entire contents of the cargo hold, plummeting to the ground a hundred feet below.

One moment the guard had been sitting there, smiling, watching the fear in the children's eyes as they stood, dotted about over the open ground in the yard, looking up at the huge ship approaching, their shovels in hand, waiting to run. The next moment the ship had stopped, and the smiling guard had vanished under a hundred tonnes of black rock which hit the ground and churned out a cloud of thick dust that spewed for yards in every direction. Then the guards were shouting and running towards the fence where their co-worker had been.

That was when he had looked back at the other children around him. Some were looking at him, and some were glancing at the fence, just yards away.

Jack remembered the realisation that crept far too slowly into his mind. No one was watching them. Thirty yards away, the dozen or so guards were either shouting at each other, or pointlessly trying to move some of the coal, even though Jack knew — everybody knew — that the man underneath was dead. Very dead. He'd seen the mess left behind when someone had been crushed.

Among the yard-workers was a one-eyed girl that

everyone called Squint, though not to her face. She was older than most by maybe two or three years, and had a temper that would spark and explode at the slightest thing. Jack had seen a fair few younger kids hit the ground after a swift slap from Squint, and often for something trivial. You didn't mess with her, you didn't cross her, and if she told you to do something then you sure as hell did it.

On that day, Squint yelled just one word at the top of her shrill voice.

"*RUN!*"

And then she took off in the direction of the fence, a second or so before every other kid. Even before Jack started to run, she was going full tilt, sprinting as fast as she could, and when Jack got to the bottom of the fence and started climbing, she was already over the top and running for the ruins.

The memory of what happened after that day was fuzzy, a blur of starved, feverish moments and nightmares, but Jack clearly remembered the last time he saw Squint alive. She turned back, just before running into an alleyway, grinned at him, and shouted. "Good luck, kiddo!"

Kiddo. She'd called everyone kiddo.

Jack still wondered what had happened to Squint,

wondered if she was still alive somewhere in the outer zone.

TALENTED

Three years before...

As the distant memory of his escape faded, Jack glanced over to the boy once more, and wondered if the child had also escaped the workhouses. There had once been a few of them dotted around the landscape not too far from the barrier, but they were all gone now, so if the boy was from a workhouse it had to be somewhere else. Jack had been back to the workhouse that he'd escaped from, many years later, only to find it deserted, though the open ground at the back of the compound was still, after years, covered in a thick black stain from the coal.

He'd often wondered why the workhouses disappeared, and thought that maybe someone had decided to move them after the mass escape that he had been involved in happened.

The boy could still have been from a workhouse, though, maybe one much further away, Jack thought, and he almost asked the child if he was an escapee, but figured that the kid would probably rather not talk about it.

The boy was called Ryan, Jack discovered that first night, as they sat opposite each other, huddled around a small campfire built from the broken remains of a door that had fallen from its hinges and lay in the middle of the floor, not far from the entrance of their new, and possibly temporary, camp. They'd moved on a dozen blocks away from Jack's old camp, as he had insisted. He liked to move regularly, but the building they found wasn't ideal, with at least three entrances open to the wind. Thankfully, the room at the back still had a door that could be shut, which allowed him to light a fire without the light being visible out on the street.

Jack had no idea where they would find new footwear for the boy, and he had nothing of a value even close to the cost of shoes to trade, but he did have some old sack cloth, which he cut and wrapped around the boy's feet. They both slept after a meagre meal of salted rat meat which Jack had traded back at The Crossing, but it took a while for Jack to drift off.

Instead he lay there, watching his new companion, listening to the boy snoring, and wondered what the hell he was going to do with the child. This was the first time in his entire life that Jack had borne the responsibility of another person on his shoulders, and if he was honest with himself, he didn't have the slightest idea how to behave. Was he supposed to teach the kid? Help him learn how to survive out here, like the old man had done for him? Obviously the boy hadn't done so well by himself, but then, when Jack thought back to his own childhood living rough, he hadn't always been lucky himself. Sometimes he had barely scratched his way through, nearly dying at least a dozen times that he could recollect. Probably more, if he actually tried to remember them all.

Maybe he *should* take the kid back to The Crossing? Maybe he should try to find someone there to take him in… no, that was utterly pointless. There wasn't a single soul in that place that wouldn't use the boy for some low purpose. Sure, there were folks there that were less terrible than most – some even showed concern for other people occasionally – but Jack could count on one hand the number of people he thought might actually try to help the kid, and not even one of those was a guarantee. The boy was his to watch over, whether he liked it or not. He could always tell Ryan to scram, to leave, but he knew that wouldn't happen, either. He'd already made the mistake of starting to warm to the boy.

It was with these troubling thoughts that sleep finally took him, drifting in on the howling wind and muffling the worry of what to do next.

In the end it turned out that he wasn't going to need to *do* anything. Only a few days in the boy's company and Jack had already gotten used to him being around. Before Jack had even realised, an entire month had passed as they moved from place to place, each time finding a good camp spot that was well hidden and then scavenging among the ruins nearby.

The boy turned out to be one of the keenest scavengers Jack had ever met, even if his first impressions of the boy's abilities were all disappointments. The kid was clumsy to begin with, not really knowing how or where to start looking, how to search a place and spot the signs of possible buried treasure. He constantly walked straight past obvious places to check, and was always surprised when Jack pointed them out. But that soon passed, and after the fourth day, while staying overnight in one of Jack's regular hideouts on the way to The Crossing to find a trader for a rubber tyre that Jack had hauled out from under a pile of collapsed masonry, Ryan crawled out from a hole underneath a smashed up kitchen unit, with a can opener in his hand.

A real, working, not even slightly rusty, can opener. The damn thing was a rare treasure, and Jack stood there for a full five minutes, turning it in his hands, inspecting the clasp joint and the circular blade. It was in perfect working condition.

"You found this… down there?" he asked, with an incredulous expression.

"Yes. Just down there," said Ryan, pointing at the hole in the floorboards that Jack wouldn't have even considered trying to squeeze into – *hadn't* considered investigating the few dozen times he had holed up in the very same room.

They were on the third floor of a derelict apartment building not too far from where Jack had seen the Hunters for the first time, an area that had been picked clean over centuries. Most days it was impossible enough to find decent salvage of any kind so close to The Crossing, and this place was less than two miles away. Collecting enough wood for a fire was a hopeless task in such a populated and over-picked area, and finding stuff like this just didn't happen.

And yet here he was, holding something that was impossible to find anymore, ever. A relic from an era that was three centuries dead.

And that wasn't the end of it.

Jack looked at the can opener, turning it over in his hands, checking for rust spots. There weren't any.

"This should be rusty," he said, frowning, and then glancing at the boy. "Just lying around in a dark,

48

probably wet place, all this time. I mean years and years. It should be rusty."

"It was in this bag," said Ryan, reaching for a clear, plastic bag lying on the floor. The bag had been ripped open, and a guilty expression crossed the boy's face. "It was in this bag, but I opened it. Sorry. I found it in the box in the wall."

Jack's eyes widened.

"What box?"

"Well. Not a box," Ryan backtracked, looking a little flustered or even embarrassed.

The boy thinks he's done wrong, Jack thought, frowning, but he let the boy continue.

"It's like a big square hole in the wall. You can't see it from the floor below. I looked. But under there," Ryan pointed at the hole in the boards, "you can crawl to the bit above the wall, and the top of the box is a bit open. The wall is cracked. I think there's more stuff in there but I can't reach any further in."

"What do you mean, there's nothing in the room where the box is?"

"I'll show you," said Ryan.

Jack followed the boy down the stairs, avoiding the piles of trash. Underneath the kitchen, on the floor below, was a large open room that Jack had walked through many times. There were two entrances, one to the stairs and the other to the front foyer of the building. But the walls were completely bare apart from occasional scraps of faded but colourful plaster.

Ryan stopped in the middle of the room and pointed at the north wall. "Right there," he said.

Jack walked over to the small hole that the boy was indicating, and peered up into the kitchen above. The same rotten and faded green cabinets could be seen through it.

"This hole wasn't here before," said Jack. "I would have seen it."

"Ah," said Ryan, looking sheepish."It kinda gave way when I first climbed inside". The child walked over to the wall below the hole, reached up, and tapped the plaster. "The box is right here, I think."

"It's hidden?" asked Jack.

"Yeah. You can check both sides. If you go under the stairs the wall is bare there as well. But the box is there. I felt it. The top had cracked open, I think, but only a little bit." The boy held up his hand, using two fingers to indicate a three inch gap. A gap just big enough for a child's hand to squeeze through. "I felt inside and it was all dry, but I couldn't pull any of the other stuff out."

Jack took out his machete and tapped the wall with the back of the blade. The sound was dull. He tapped the area a foot away, and the sound changed.

It was hollow.

"My god. There must be a safe hidden in there."

And there was. After five minutes of hacking at the aged and softened plaster, which crumbled and fell away in large chunks, Jack took a step back and stared at the secure door of a metal safe, his mouth open. He didn't know what to say, and was utterly dumbfounded. No one found stuff like this anymore.

Ten minutes later and they had used Jack's wrench to pull the kitchen cabinets from the wall on the floor above, and pull up the floorboards, then prised open the top of the safe. The metal was a colour that Jack had rarely seen before. New metal. And worth a lot to trade for. It might take a while for him to pull the damn thing out of the wall and break it up, but metal that wasn't rusty was valuable.

The safe turned out to be mostly full of paper. Currency from centuries ago that was absolutely worthless now, except for the material it was made of. But inside they also found boxes of marker pens that still worked, a bunch of wax crayons, and some faded photographs. But on top of the pile of paper, pinning everything down, was a box of tools. Screwdrivers, cutting knives, a hammer, a chisel set, and more – all of them in immaculate condition. Jack sat in the middle of the room, the tools in his hands, speechless once more. This hoard of treasure was the most valuable he had ever found.

That night they moved camps again, away from the place that they had made so much noise when Jack first hauled the safe out of the wall and then broke it apart. They hid in the cellar storeroom of a collapsed shop two blocks up, hoping that it was far enough away that if someone went looking and even found the recent disturbance, they wouldn't be able to track who had made it.

When Jack awoke the next morning, there were scrawled crayon pictures across the back wall of the cellar, near where Ryan was sleeping – stick-men of various colours, and there in the middle was one tall figure and a smaller figure, holding hands.

HUNTED

The thought of those pictures stirred something, a hurt that hadn't gone away even after nearly two years. He couldn't wait any longer, and quickly struggled out of the pile of rags, pushed aside the wardrobe doors and fell out onto the floor. He smashed his shoulder on the ground and winced with pain, but then ignored it as he lay there, staring across the room at the corner where the magazines should be, at the spot that was now empty. He stumbled forward, scrambling in the darkness, hunting for anything that may have been left behind, but the corner was empty, the magazines gone – including the one that Ryan had drawn his stick-men in the day that *they* had taken him.

Jack had always worried – back then, when he had been travelling with the boy – that one day they would be caught in a raid. He'd worried about how the boy would react, if he would cry out in fear and give them both away.

And he'd tried to explain to the boy.

IF THEY COME

Two years before...

Months before, during the cold season when they were sitting around a low burning campfire in a warehouse in the old docklands, he had told the boy how to behave if the Hunters came and found them. It was bitter cold on that night, and they were both wrapped up in dusty, mould-riddled chunks of carpet, stripped from an office two floors above. The carpet stank of the ages, but it kept the chilling breeze, which gusted in through the massive holes in the building, at bay.

The fire was barely alive, smouldering, but still managing a visible glow that lit the interior of the tiny loading bay area that Jack had chosen. Lighting a fire anywhere else would alert passersby that they were there, but the overhang of the bay, and the metal stairs that they were huddled under, hid the light of the fire well enough. Jack still barely slept through the night, unhappy that they hadn't found somewhere to barricade themselves away, but he had to admit the warmth of the fire was a rare gift during the winter months.

He didn't know why he chose to speak of the Hunters for the first time on that occasion. The boy had been with him for nearly a year and the subject hadn't come up at all. But then — they hadn't seen Hunters in all that time. Moving from place to place in search of salvage or food further out in the outer zone did have its benefits, even though they were often weighted against dangers.

"If they come," he had said, and paused for a minute, wondering if the boy even knew about the raids. "If the Hunters ever find us, you are to stay hidden, and quiet."

Jack didn't look at the boy as he spoke, but he could sense his gaze upon him. Even after nearly a year he was still a quiet child. Sometimes he would talk, but it was always about what they had unearthed that day, or what they could make out of the things that they found, even though the boy knew that their goal was mostly to trade the stuff in for supplies. When he did get going he would chatter non-stop for a while, and big plans of constructing flying ships or boats, or fortresses, would spill out.

But most of the time he was quiet.

"Do you understand?" Jack asked, finally looking up at Ryan.

Ryan nodded, but didn't speak. His gaze shifted between Jack and the wavering glow of the fire.

"Do you know who I am speaking of?" Jack asked. "The Hunters. The soldiers that come in the great ships and take people away. Do you know of those?"

"Yes," Ryan finally replied. "I've seen them."

"You have?" He was curious. The boy had never spoken of where he had come from before, even though he had asked questions. Ryan always clammed up, stopped talking, and Jack had taken the hint after a few attempts to at prising the information from the child.

Ryan smiled, but it wasn't a cheerful one. "Before the people who took my shoes," he said, "I hid from the soldiers in the street, but they weren't in a big ship. They were in a truck. I don't know who they were looking for, but they found someone and took them away. I was hiding over the street and they saw me. I ran and ran, and that's when I ran into the people who took my shoes."

He looked down at the boots that they had traded for. After finding the stash in the safe, Jack had made it a priority to get the boy new shoes, and it had cost dearly, but had been worth it.

"These are much betterer boots," said Ryan. "They

56

keep my feet warm."

"Better. Not betterer," Jack said, with a grin.

"Better," Ryan echoed.

"Well, then you know what they do. The Hunters? They hunt people down and take them. And if they find us — find me — you are to stay hidden and quiet. Do you get that?"

Another nod.

"You can't give yourself away, or cry out. If you do that then they will find you, too."

They sat in silence for a while.

"Then I would be alone," Ryan said, which took Jack by surprise. He hadn't considered that a child so young could think of such things.

"Well, you'll be alone one day anyway," Jack replied before even thinking about how morbid and pessimistic it would sound. "I'm much older than you, and I will get very old, one day. Too old to travel any longer."

More silence.

"You hide," Jack repeated. "And you stay hidden if they come. No noise, and maybe they won't find you."

HUNTED

After two years, Jack still preferred *betterer* to *better.*

He sat in the dust and mould of the apartment, staring at the blank space where the magazines had been just a few minutes before, and listened to the distant sounds of the Hunters heading back to their vehicles. He could feel anger building up, burning in his gut.

An urge to follow the Hunters and take back what was his.

But what good would that achieve? he thought. *They will just take you.* He knew that no matter how angry he felt, how vengeful, he wouldn't get up and follow them. He wouldn't because he hadn't done it before. He knew that he was a coward, just as he had been *that* night.

LOST

Two years before...

Jack stood over the boy, towering above him, his voice raised, as he let the anger flood out. He didn't hit the kid, even though for the briefest of moments that urge surfaced. *How dare he? This child that I've taken in and fed, and kept alive? How dare he draw his damn stick-men in one of my magazines?*

Jack looked down at the magazine, at the colourful pictures of the streets of the city whose glory was three centuries dead, and at the stick-men that now stood in the street, crayon drawings that Ryan had probably thought would make the place look more real.

And he shouted, not even trying to be wary of others nearby, and the risk of drawing attention.

But then, after a few minutes, he stopped. The boy was staring at the ground, his face flushed bright red with shame. Jack didn't know what had possessed the child with the idea of drawing in his magazine, but he could see clearly that the boy regretted it. As the flush of anger passed, Jack suddenly felt foolish. What was he doing? Why was he shouting at the one person in the world that trusted him and would follow him anywhere? All over a damn magazine? Hell, it was the latest in his collection, and *the damn boy had found it for him*. He had come running out of the ruin of the old shop with a huge grin on his face.

And there he was, scolding the child. Suddenly the foolish feeling turned to shame, much stronger shame than the boy must have been feeling. He put his hand on Ryan's shoulder and spoke just two words...

"Sorry... I..."

...before the roar of the Dropship engines cut the air around them, and the *whump* of the boosters almost rocked the building they were standing in as it hit the ground nearby.

Jack remembered panicking and darting for the darkened room behind them, heading for their makeshift bolt-hole to hide, expecting the boy to be right behind him. But as he heard the crashing of the doors on the floor below them as they were kicked in, and the smashing of the one remaining window, Jack turned and saw that the boy was not there.

Where the hell had he gone? Where was the *damn* boy? Jack panicked, looking around, but then he heard the thud of boots on the stairs and realised that the Hunters were upon them, and that in just seconds they would both be caught.

He turned and ran for the bolt-hole, hoping that Ryan had found cover and was already hiding, but Jack didn't make it to the hole in the floor of the small side-room as the door to the main room crashed open and grey-clad Hunters burst in. Jack darted to the side and crouched behind the rotten and torn sofa at the back of the room, knowing even then, as his hands went to his side, ready to draw his machetes, that the Hunters would find him.

But seconds passed, and the Hunters didn't come into the side-room. Jack could see around the edge of the sofa that they had moved into the back rooms, where the old pantry and kitchen were, where Ryan must have run.

Don't let them find the boy, he thought. *Please don't let them find...*

A Hunter emerged from the room, pushing Ryan ahead of him. The boy was hustled into the middle of the room as the four Hunters encircled him.

Now, thought Jack. *Go now, while they aren't looking. Attack them from behind. You'll get the drop on them, and there's a chance, isn't there? There's a chance that you could take one of them out, grab his gun, and shoot the others.*

But you don't know how to fire the gun, do you? he

thought. *You won't be able to fight them all off.*

He watched, hesitating, hopelessly not acting at the one moment that he knew he should.

But then the boy was shaking his head.

They're talking to him, he thought. *They're asking him something. What are they asking him?*

He heard a voice, low, one of the Hunters. "No one else here? Are you sure?"

The boy shook his head again.

And then it was too late. The Hunters ushered Ryan out of the room and into the hall, and were gone.

Seconds too late, Jack jumped from his hiding place behind the ruined sofa and ran through the rooms of their hideout, rushing down the hall as he drew his machetes, hurrying out into the street only to see the windowless vehicle heading away at an incredible speed, then turning a corner a block away.

Then it was gone. And so was Ryan.

TIME TO GO

And the boy did exactly as you told him, didn't he? He didn't give you up, he kept quiet. When all along you thought that your instructions might keep him alive if ever you were caught, that he would stay silent and hide, you never expected it to be the other way round, did you?

You didn't act that night because you were a coward, Jack told himself. You didn't act and the boy was taken — Ryan was gone — leaving you to stew over it again and again, every night for two years, to wake up sweating, crying like a fool.

What were you expecting after he was gone? That you could get over it?

In the darkness of the room, in the spot where the magazines had been, Jack finally realised what it was he must do. He'd waited too long — much too long — even though he'd always known what his only real option was. Two years ago the boy had been taken by the Hunters, and for two years Jack had tried to reason with himself, screwed his head up with thoughts of what he could have done — should have done — on that night, but he had never, until that moment, accepted that there was a choice he could make that might give him a chance to get back what was lost.

Jack Avery stood up and walked towards the door.

PICKUP

Corporal Markell stood watch at the rear of the Armoured Personnel Vehicle as the last of the new workforce recruits were pushed inside. The corporal then nodded at the last squad as they passed by with no new prisoners in tow. They wouldn't be berated for not bringing someone back this time. This whole trip out had been low-yield, as her superior officer, Lieutenant Cray had suggested it would be.

It was pointless going back to the same area after such a short amount of time, and Cray had said as much when the target location had been announced an hour before. But they all knew that disputing the target was pointless, and even if they did it would be them that would catch the blame for the lack of worker harvest.

Markell closed the back door and turned to head for the side of the vehicle, glad that the day's fiasco was over and that they could all go back to their dorms and watch TV, and maybe get drunk.

But there was a figure standing just feet away, in the middle of the street — a man that shouldn't have been there. Markell frowned, and slowly raised the Assault

Rifle.

The man lifted two machetes from his belt, held his hands out, and just as Markell was about to fire, the man – who looked tired and weak – dropped the machetes to the ground.

The man was giving himself up. It was a ridiculous notion, Markell thought. No one ever gave themselves up.

"We have another prisoner," stammered Markell into the radio, still not quite accepting the man's actions. Was he mad? He must be – had to be – to make such a stupid choice. It just wasn't done. Seconds later, the last squad rushed around the truck and encircled the man as Markell opened the back of the vehicle and watched, stunned, as the man voluntarily walked forward, heading for the open maw of the truck.

Markell frowned again as the man stopped at the back of the truck and turned. The man said something, but Markell couldn't hear him clearly. The words were muffled by the helmet's padding.

No one ever gave themselves up willingly, Markell thought again. Why would they? Even life out here in the ruins was better than the short life of a work slave, Markell knew that. Yet, here was this man doing just that, the first to do so in seven years of Markell's military career.

Markell felt a sudden urge to speak to the man, and it was uncontrollable.

I must know why.

INTO DARKNESS

Jack stood at the back of the prison vehicle, about to step up into the open door, but then he turned to the nearest Hunter, the one who had been at the back of the truck as he had approached. He looked at the Hunter directly where his eyes should be – or Jack's nearest guess – and asked. "Who are you people?"

Then, to his shock, the Hunter reached up and tapped the side of his helmet, which immediately gave a hiss of compressed air before the entire front visor opened upwards.

Staring back at him, from within the armour of a Hunter, was the face of a young woman. He couldn't guess her age exactly, but thought she could be no older than twenty-five, thirty at most.

Then the Hunter spoke, and she sounded as he had expected, just like a young woman. This wasn't a robot, or something worse. Hunters were just people.

"Why give yourself up?" asked Corporal Lisa Markell, ignoring the furious chatter on the radio, and the orders to raise her protective mask, *immediately*.

Jack hesitated, and then looked at the woman. "I

have to find a boy that you took from me," he said, just before he was pushed into the vehicle by one of the other Hunters.

The back doors of the prison vehicle closed and he was plunged into darkness.

I was right, thought Jack. *You can't see out of these things. Shame I can't tell anyone that.*

WHY

The vehicle sped through the streets, rapidly heading towards the Dropship, and in the middle compartment – the section of each vehicle that contained the recruitment squad and their equipment – Lisa pulled off her helmet and threw it to the floor.

"Are you mad?" asked Johnson, another corporal in her section. "You *never* take your helmet off. 101, man!"

"I had to know why," answered Lisa.

Johnson looked confused. "You'll be lucky if they don't demote you for it," he said.

"I had to know why he gave himself up," Lisa continued. "It just didn't make any sense. No one does that. *Ever.*"

"Of course not," said Johnson. "Even the irradiated scum out here aren't *that* stupid."

Johnson paused for a moment. "Why did he do it, anyway?" he asked.

Lisa looked over at Johnson, and smiled. "He wants to find a boy that was captured."

"Oh. Well, tough luck on that one," said Johnson,

shuffling in his seat and then roughly snapping the safety belt into place. "They all die within a month or two, anyway."

CAUGHT

Complete darkness surrounded Jack as he sat on the hard ground inside the back of the prison vehicle. Around him he could hear movement, and a soft whimpering came from somewhere nearby.

Over near the back of the compartment, he thought.

Other prisoners.

Some of them afraid like you are.

All of them afraid like you are.

Jack took a few deep, rhythmic breaths, calming his nerves and attempting to steady himself as the vehicle tore along the streets, leaving behind everything he had known.

He wondered if he would ever see the ruins again, ever visit The Crossing, and he realised that he didn't really care. The life he was leaving behind held nothing for him anymore, probably never had. It had been a life and that was all it amounted to.

Survival.

Except some parts, and all of that was either gone forever, dead, or somewhere, he hoped, in his future.

This.

This was all that was left.

His search for Ryan had resumed. After two long years of wondering, he had finally given up and actually done something. He'd taken a step towards the unknown, but he knew this was where Ryan had gone and where he needed to follow, even if he never found the boy again. If this turned out to be a journey that ended only in his death, then at least he would know something, wouldn't he? At least he could die knowing that he had tried, even if it had taken him two years to commit himself to act.

Jack sat in the darkness, listening to the noises around him, and swore that as long as he lived he would task himself with two things only – he would find Ryan, and somehow he would make up for failing the boy when he had been needed most. Jack knew that he could have done little when the Hunters took Ryan, and he knew that he would probably have died in the attempt, but somehow that seemed to him to be better than sitting there and just letting them take him.

This was what he went through, back then. What Ryan went through after he was taken, and you were left standing in the road, just watching the vehicles speed away.

The darkness, the frightened noises made by the other prisoners, and the not knowing where the truck was heading to.

Now you know this much.

The vehicle turned a corner, violently throwing everyone stuck in the dark prison at the back onto the floor. They sprawled over each other, grasping out at nothing, at anything, just trying to steady themselves. Hands pushed into faces and feet kicked up as people struggled desperately. There were cries of fear as the vehicle swerved again, skidded and then continued on a straight path. For a few seconds the heaving mass of bodies writhed over each other until finally everyone had settled back on the floor again.

Jack tried to picture the streets outside in his mind, playing back the turns they had made, and the directions they were travelling in, and estimated that they were now four blocks from his hideout, four entire blocks in what? A minute? The confusion as the vehicle had turned the corner had thrown his orientation out for a moment, but his mind raced to catch up, to estimate their location.

The roar of the engine brought more cries of fear from the other passengers around him. He tried to guess how many people were in the back with him but it was impossible. The darkness inside the armoured truck was absolute. There was not even the slightest glimmer of light that might allow his eyes to adjust. He could see no shadows or other figures but he could smell them, and that wasn't very pleasant.

Most people living in the Outer Zone, in the ruins of the old city, didn't get to bathe very often. Some of them never. Fresh water was a rare commodity and was more than often used for drinking. There were water springs in various places, but they were guarded by gangs, or were in the centre of one of the hovels that littered the ruins, and never out in the open or in a place that was accessible to just anyone. Of all the things that were considered valuable in the Outer Zone, clean water was among the highest.

And right then Jack would do anything for a drink.

He thought of Ryan again, and how the boy must have felt making this journey. This was frightening even to Jack, who wasn't disturbed by many things after such a long time in the ruins. But to a boy, this must have been terrifying.

Someone shoved him onto his back and Jack felt a large figure move past him, as whoever it was struggled to their feet, and then there was a roar of annoyance.

"Where the hell am I?" boomed the gruff voice of a man Jack figured must have been unconscious for the journey so far. Jack couldn't place it, but way back and hidden in his mind somewhere, that voice was familiar.

When no answer came, the man pushed forward, and though Jack couldn't see what was going on, he heard others crying out as the man unleashed his fury on them. Jack was just sitting up when a heavy weight landed upon him. Another man — or a woman — struggled and rolled over him as Jack pushed them off, trying not to push so hard that he would injure the person. It wasn't a courtesy that most would give but he saw no reason to increase the suffering of those around him. It was as bad for them as it was for him. Worse even.

At least he had volunteered.

"Let me out, you—" the man bellowed, but he was cut off as the vehicle swerved sharply around another corner. Jack heard a loud thud on the side of the vehicle, and then another loud thud, a grunt, and then silence. Jack thought that in the second impact he had heard a cracking noise, like small bones breaking.

Unconscious again, thought Jack, as the vehicle quickly swerved, this time to the left. The fool, whoever this man with the familiar voice was, had been standing with nothing to hold on to, and nothing to counter the gravity of the swerving vehicle. At least he wouldn't beat on anyone else for a while.

He went back to the movement and speed of the vehicle. Trying to adjust his bearings once more.

We're into 342nd Street. And now we're passing the old rail station.

And still the vehicle sped onwards.

We're getting close to the old pits and the open ground not far from the rail station.

And that was where once, when Jack had been much younger, the slave baron Jagan had kept his camp. It had been where the pit fights, a dark time in Jack's life, had taken place. A time he tried hard to forget about.

The vehicle slowed, then almost halted, but then Jack's stomach lurched as it shot upwards, as though climbing a hill.

No hills here. So where were they going now? Had he missed something?

But he wasn't sure. His mind scrambled over the terrain, recalling everything in the area, searching for a section of high ground. But he knew there was nothing for the vehicle to climb up like this, unless...

We're going into the Dropship.

We must be. There are no hills in this area, only pits. Pits full of the bones of Jagan's Gladiators. That would be a good place for something as large as the Dropship to land.

All that open space.

The vehicle moved slowly now, as though navigating narrow lanes with care, turning left, then right, and then finally stopping. There were more cries of fear from the other passengers, but Jack sat in silence, thinking only of Ryan.

If the boy could survive this, get through it all, then I can. All I need to do is keep my nerves steady, stay calm.

Breathe.

Whatever happens next, none of it matters if it means I end up in the place where Ryan is, or at least where he was two years ago.

They won't kill us, surely?

Would they? It was possible, wasn't it? But that would be ridiculous. Why would they go to so much trouble to round up people only to kill them?

Unless they did kill people, maybe the weak ones, he thought. That was also a possibility.

But you're not weak, are you? Maybe some of these others are, and they will die, but you're still strong. Getting older, and prone to coughs in bad weather, but still strong. And the boy had been strong, always had been, even though he was slight of build. Ryan had proven time and again that he wasn't as weak as Jack had first thought when he saw him sitting on the sidewalk the day they met. As soon as the boy had been fed a few times he'd started to become less gaunt and more human. And even though he was still thin, there had been a grittiness to him, a stubbornness that wasn't just in his attitude.

A thought cut through the silence.

Ryan would be nine years old now. He wouldn't be as small as he had been back then. He could even be a foot taller. He'd surely be more lean and muscular. He always was a strong kid.

As a hissing noise filled the darkness around him, and a faint mustard smell entered his nostrils, Jack's mind went back once more looking for somewhere to hide, to a time when they had been together.

Like a father and son. That's also what he had thought the day they celebrated Ryan's birthday that first time.

ANT SOUP

Two Years Before

They'd celebrated Ryan's birthday on the anniversary of the day that Jack found him. It was the only day that Jack could use, because Ryan couldn't remember when his birthday was.

"My parents always told me when my birthday was," Ryan had said when Jack first asked him as they sat on the flat edge of a warehouse loading bay. "I never thought about it."

It seemed that an even colder winter than usual was on its way. At least that was how it appeared to Jack. The bitter, cold wind was early by several weeks, and although they had supplies stashed it wouldn't be enough to last the entire three months of bad weather to come. Jack had known then that they would have to resort to trading something that he didn't want to part with or they'd be hunting rats. But it wasn't turning just yet, not quite.

He thought, as they sat there looking out over the expanse of ruins that was the Far Reaches, a place further out from the middle of the city than Jack liked to go, that they'd manage, they would get by, and he was determined to enjoy the last of the fading summer before the snow drifts came.

Every year, when the weather was just turning cold after the blistering weeks of heat that marked the summer months, the ants came out. It always happened at the same time of year. They'd come bursting from the ground, spewing tiny piles of dirt along the gutters and out of the cracks in the broken roads. And there were millions of them. For a day or so the air was filled with flying ants. They got everywhere, even in his clothes and his hair.

Their arrival marked the end of the hot weather and the creeping in of the autumn and the long winter that would bring about the deaths of so many. With little fuel, and nowhere to hide from the chilling winds and the unforgiving snow that would follow, many in the outer areas of the city would perish. Two days before he'd found the boy, he'd been heating a pan of squashed ants over a fire. It had been that time.

You'd think they'd taste foul, but they don't, he thought. With a bit of added mint and some water, they made a broth that tasted as sweet as the sugar that he remembered from his childhood, though Jack knew that memory was probably not as accurate as he believed.

The first time that he'd eaten ant stew, sitting next to a similar fire, many miles away and a lot of years before, he'd turned the offered cup away, finding the idea foul and the withered old man sitting opposite him even more disgusting. The old man had laughed at him, calling him a fool and telling Jack that he'd soon change his mind. And that old grisly fellow had been right.

Jack was amused to see the very same reaction from the boy even as Jack gulped down a whole cup of the dirty, brown, steaming broth. And he was even more amused a few minutes later when Ryan's growling, empty stomach made the boy change his mind.

It had been just the same for me, thought Jack.

As he'd watched Ryan grimace with the first sip, then look surprised and gulp it down, an idea hit Jack. It was almost exactly a year that they'd been travelling together, which meant it was sort of Ryan's birthday.

And that meant that there needed to be some sort of celebration, somehow. Jack had no clue what he would do for the boy, but he was damn sure that he was going to do something.

CAUGHT

The memory of that day faded as the mustard smell filled his nostrils. He tried to cover his face but knew it was pointless. There would be no vent in the back of the vehicle and he already knew that.

Gas, he thought. *This is what they do to people that they've caught.* He knew that at some point they would want to take everybody off the vehicle, and other than forcing them to move and possibly using violence, the easiest way would be to gas them all out. He wondered for a moment why he was even bothering to cover his mouth. The gas was so thick in the enclosed space that there was no escaping it.

Around him, the cries of fear returned, and the sound of coughing pierced the darkness as people succumbed to the gas. Yet he still held his breath, thinking the same mantra that the old man had taught him, over and over. Slow and shallow. Slow and shallow. He pushed his hand against his hood, using it to filter the air. And he knew it was working, to some degree, but not enough. Bright sparkles of light flickered across his vision, stark in contrast to the darkness around him. He started to feel faint and slightly sickened. He wouldn't throw up but the dizzying effect of the gas made him feel drunk.

Eventually the coughing and the cries of those around him ceased, and he knew that he was the only one still conscious. Everyone else in the back of the truck had fallen. And there was something else familiar about all this. He tried to recall when he had felt it before.

Just as his eyes started to close, and his body began to collapse into a deep unconsciousness, Jack remembered the sharp sting of the dart that the slaver had used.

THE PITS

Many Years Before

Jagan was a name that for many years struck terror into the hearts of every living soul that lived in the Outer Zone. He went by other names, but Jagan was what the people of The Crossing had called the slave baron who ruled from his throne in the open grounds east of 342nd Street.

Jack had seen him from a distance several times during his days in the pits, and was always in awe of the man's imposing figure. He was easily seven feet tall and was a mountain of pale muscle covered with armour that Jack thought might have been captured from the Hunters. He wore his bright red hair tied in a single braid that hung down his back, and even from a distance you could see his angry eyes glaring outwards at those he commanded.

The day that Jack had been caught, back when he wasn't even twenty years old, he had left The Crossing after trading and was heading out into the ruins to find a new spot to set up. He'd turned a corner and found a dozen heavily armed men walking towards him. Their armour was hotchpotch, made up of some pieces of the grey battle gear of the Hunters and mixed up with battered pieces of metal. The leading man, who had to be as tall as Jagan himself, wore armour that Jack thought was made from cut up street signs, and he carried a long heavy metal pole with the word STOP on the metal plate at the end.

He remembered seeing the wagon behind the men, pulled along by a dozen or more gaunt figures, but that was all he'd managed to see before he felt the sharp sting in his left shoulder. He'd looked down and seen a throwing dart sticking out of his clothing, and then he looked back up at the approaching group.

When he awoke he was in the back of the wagon, tied to the metal railings. He had been stripped down to just the t-shirt he wore under his coats and the bottommost pair of jeans. Everything else was gone.

GLASS HALF-EMPTY

Corporal Lisa Markell stared down at the plate of food on the table in front of her and decided that she wasn't hungry. It wasn't that the food was bad — quite the opposite, in fact. The RAD — Reconnaissance and Acquisition Division — the section of the Inner Zone's armed forces that was tasked with the security of all salvage and workforce recruitment operations, and of which she had been a member of her entire adult life, fed their people well.

Too well, some said. The plate in front of her was loaded with carbohydrates and high protein, including meat, which was a rare treat, even for the wealthy who lived inside the barrier, and she felt a pang of guilt as she pushed it away.

"You not eating that?" a voice asked, and Lisa looked up to see Johnson eyeing the plate hungrily. They'd only been sat down for a few minutes and his plate was already empty.

"Help yourself," Lisa said and pushed the plate across to him.

Her thoughts had been miles away, not paying attention to the hum of activity around her as hundreds of RAD officers and troopers huddled around the long tables in the mess hall, ravenously filling their stomachs. Or more specifically, her mind had been back in the Outer Zone, where she was standing behind the truck as the troopers in her squad climbed back into the armoured personnel carrier after finishing the task of loading the small catch of recruits.

And the man had come out of nowhere, she thought, just appearing a few feet away from her. He stood motionless, watching her and looking behind her into the back of the truck where the captives were.

That had been half an hour ago, and she was still mulling it over. It bothered her. There was something about the way the man looked past her into the darkness of the back of the truck that unnerved her. Unlike almost everyone captured by their raids, this man hadn't been afraid of her or her troops. She had seen it in his eyes. No fear. And he had just walked up to them, silently, and given himself up.

He'd volunteered.

It had been a first for her, and from what Johnson and the other corporals had said, it was almost unknown for someone to just give themselves up like that. She imagined what she and her troops must look like to those who lived in the ruins. Grey armour over black jumpsuits, a black visor blocking all view of the person inside. When Lisa had first looked in a mirror after donning her battle gear, she had thought that she was looking at someone else. The armour was made to strip all individuality from the person wearing it and was customised to fit. Male, female, thin, bulky — none of those features were obvious from the outside.

The armour was even made to look imposing — frightening even. And it worked for the vast majority of those facing off against them. Sure, sometimes a group of Scavs or some remnant of the old Slave Empire would be among the buildings they were raiding, and they would fight back, but even they had learned to fear the RAD raiders.

Yet this man had calmly given himself up and even climbed into the back of the truck without being pushed or forced. And he'd had the nerve to speak to her.

And she couldn't get that out of her head.

"What's eating you?" asked Ellard, another corporal, currently sitting to her right.

Across from Lisa, Johnson stopped eating and grinned. "She got spooked by one of the recruits we picked up."

Lisa looked up, narrowing her eyes at Johnson.

"I didn't get spooked," she said, frowning with

irritation.

Johnson shrugged and went back to eating, but Lisa wasn't letting it go that easily. He'd annoyed her. She turned to Ellard. "This...recruit... He just walked up to us and gave himself in."

Ellard frowned. "No way," he said before shovelling in another mouthful of food. "Must be a crazy."

Possibly, thought Lisa. But she had seen the man's eyes. And she had caught a lot of crazies in her time, and this guy wasn't one of them. There had been determination there, she had seen it.

Lisa stood up, pushing her chair back, and left the rest of her comrades to their meal. She knew she'd have to be ready for the Dropship to land at the base in twenty minutes, and be ready to process her catch at the import facility, but that still gave her a few minutes to head back to squad's ready room. And there would be no one else there.

Two minutes later she shut the door behind her and walked over to the console on the wall at the far end. She hit the catch on the wall below the computer terminal, waited for the seat to pop out of the wall, and sat down. With one tap the terminal came to life, flickering a few times before displaying the identification screen. A flash of green light swept across her face as the terminal identified her before the familiar view of dozens of info panels appeared.

Lisa stared at the screen.

What the hell am I even doing? she thought.

He'd been looking for a boy.

Lisa tapped the screen and pulled up the roster of recruits, shaking her head as she wondered why she was even bothering.

27, 334.

She narrowed the search, selecting filters for juvenile, and male.

5,723.

Lisa stared at the number and frowned. Had there really been so many captured? More than five thousand? Lisa narrowed the search again, selecting only those still alive.

2341.

More than half of them were dead.

Again she questioned what she was doing. There was no way she was going to find the boy that the man was looking for. *Stupid*, she thought. *I don't even have a name or age.*

The door at the other end of the ready room opened

and several of the troops in her squad filed in. Lisa tapped the screen, quickly logging off, stood up and hit the button on the wall that would tuck the console and the seat back into the wall.

As the noise of her fellow RAD members resounded off the walls, she thought about the numbers again.

More than half were dead.

CAUGHT

The huge man hit the ground with a grunt, kicking up a cloud of sand and dust from the dry earth. And then he lay there, twitching, as three of the Hunters circled him and then began to drag him away.

Jack squinted, his eyes trying to adjust to the bright sunlight while still attempting to take in the utter chaos around him. Hundreds of captives were standing in groups dotted around the massive yard, most of them, like him, still groggy from the gas, and most of them still and placid. But the huge man in his group, the one Jack thought had become rowdy in the back of the carrier, was now sporting a smashed nose, which looked like someone had hit him with a hammer, and was not co-operating at all. No sooner had he come round, just after Jack, than he was up, roaring and bellowing, and charging towards the nearest Hunter.

Must be an ex-slaver.

The man was smaller than Jack had estimated, probably only a few inches taller than he was, but he was broader in the shoulders and far more muscular. Jack was impressed. The man even managed to get a hit in on one of the Hunters, smashing his fist into the side of the trooper's helmet and knocking him down, before the buzz of shock-sticks cut through the air and three other Hunters descended on him, jabbing at him with the crackling weapons.

As Jack's eyes began to re-adjust to the bright sunlight, he managed to take in his surroundings. They were in some kind of port facility. Huge, grey concrete buildings rose around them on all sides, and the ground was mostly dry dirt apart from the concrete platform that the Dropship had landed upon.

Jack looked back at the armoured vehicle they had just been dragged from and along the line of other vehicles. There were a lot more of them than he had expected, and he estimated that at least thirty of the armoured carriers had driven off the Dropship.

And so many Hunters, he thought. There had to be hundreds of them.

He watched as other groups of captives were dragged, unconscious, from the backs of the carriers and unceremoniously dumped on the dry dirt. Some of the other captives were starting to come round, easing slowly out of their drugged state and standing up, looking around and appearing as confused as he felt.

Jack's gaze drifted back to the huge angry guy being dragged away. The three Hunters hauled him a hundred yards across the hard ground and then dumped him onto some kind of moving metal platform. The unconscious body lay still as the moving platform carried it away into one of the buildings. He looked up at the sign at the front of the building, which read Conversion Screening Facility, and wondered what that meant.

Then Jack noticed the Hunter watching him from ten yards away and he lowered his head, staring down at the barren ground.

Don't give them any trouble. Just stay silent and still, unassuming. But he glanced up one last time at the building where the big guy had been taken. He didn't like the sound of conversion, even though he had no idea what that meant.

The Hunter was still watching him intently, and Jack felt himself involuntarily clenching his hands together, shifting uncomfortably, and looking around at the other people in the same group. He recognised only two of them, an older man and woman that he had seen several times entering or leaving the same building that he had been staying in when he had surrendered to the Hunters. They were a couple, he thought, and lived somewhere on the upper floors of the building. Dozens of others had lived there, each staking their own claim on one of the floors in some corner where no one else was, but just like everywhere else, they tended to keep to themselves and protect what was theirs. Apart from places like The Crossing, where he often went to trade, there were very few communities in the Outer Zone.

No one trusted anyone else.

"Everybody up," said a metallic sounding voice from a few feet away. Jack turned and saw that it was the Hunter that had been watching him. At that command, several other Hunters approached and encircled the group, which Jack could now see was actually only made up of twenty or so people. The Hunters were waving their shock-sticks and pointing in the direction of another large building directly ahead of them. As they started walking forward, guided by the rough hands of the Hunters, Jack noticed the other groups lined up in the yard were also being told to stand. But his group was the first.

It wasn't the Conversion Facility that they were heading for, and Jack was grateful for that, but as the troupe of bedraggled refugees was ushered through the massive concrete doors of the building and into a large open space with white painted markings on the floor, Jack began to feel uneasy.

There were twenty or more entrances leading off one side of the room, and every one of them led into a brightly-lit tunnel. In front of each entrance was a booth with another Hunter sat in it, and next to that, some kind of metal platform roughly three feet across. The Hunter that had been watching Jack pushed him forward so that he was the third in the queue that was now forming.

In front of him were the old couple, and as Jack watched, one of the Hunters urged the man forward. The old guy was hesitant at first, but the Hunter pointed at the platform and, with a flick of his wrist, the shock-stick in his hand hummed to life. Next to Jack, the old woman cried out, telling the old man to go, but the man looked back at her, worried.

"Go," she said, her voice shrill. "Or they'll hurt you."

The man stepped up onto the platform and stood still, looking around at the hundreds of captives now being forced to stand in lines in front of the booths and platforms.

A flash of light almost blinded Jack as the platform flickered to life. Blue lights flowed around the base of the metal panel, swirling clockwise around it until, a few seconds later, the lights turned green. From nearby came a buzzing sound, and Jack looked over to the tunnels that led out of the huge hall. Two tunnels along from where they were queued, a tunnel had lit up green, matching the colour on the platform.

The old man still stood on the platform, confused, and Jack could empathise with him. What the hell did all this mean? What were the platforms for? His heart jumped as the old man was pushed off the platform. The old guy looked at the Hunter that had pushed him, both fear and a hint of anger, maybe even defiance, crossing his face, but the Hunter pointed at the green-lit tunnel, and the old man looked back at the old lady once more and then started to trudge towards the tunnel.

Next, the old woman stepped up onto the platform, and no sooner had the blue lights started flickering than they changed to a flashing red. At this, the Hunter nearest the old woman pointed towards the corridor next to the one the old man had walked down. The old woman stepped off the platform and started to walk towards the second corridor, but as she approached, she looked back and then quickly headed towards the same corridor that the old man had taken. Two Hunters rushed forward and blocked her path, pointing her to the red corridor. She hesitated, but in the end she complied and started to walk down the tunnel they'd directed her to.

As Jack stepped forward, heading towards the platform, he glanced across the line of corridor entrances, and saw that they alternated in colour –

green, red, green, red and so on. People were being led into a corridor depending on which colour the platform indicated. As he stepped up onto the platform, Jack noticed a young man being directed down the green corridor, and on the next booth another older man, who could barely walk, was being sent down the red.

Jack heard a buzzing noise and felt the platform under his feet vibrate for a moment, and he looked down.

A young man and an old man had gone down the green corridor. The old woman and a nearly crippled man had gone down the red. This had to mean something, thought Jack. Was the platform some kind of decision maker? A technology that could somehow choose who went where? And what were the criteria? Two healthy people down one corridor, and two unhealthy ones down the next.

As Jack looked down, he hoped that the platform would be lit up green and was relieved when it was. He stepped off the platform and started walking towards the corridor with the green archway, and since none of the Hunters tried to stop him, or guide him the other way, he thought that he must have guessed correctly.

The corridor went on for roughly a hundred yards, and was lit on both sides by bright fluorescent lights spaced ten feet apart. The ground was smooth and worn, like many feet had trodden the path that Jack now walked, and he only looked back once as he headed along it. Ahead of him, roughly fifty feet away, was the old man who had gone into the tunnel first and beyond that, near the end of the corridor, he saw the back of the young man moving swiftly away. He had stopped and was leaning against the wall. As Jack approached, he slowed down and stopped next to the man.

"You okay?" he asked. He found it strange to be asking after someone else's wellbeing for what seemed the first time in years. Other than when he met the boy, Ryan, Jack hadn't given much thought to others. After all, no one ever did for him.

The old man was breathing heavily and clutching his chest. My...chest." said the man, his voice strained. "It hurts."

Jack stood there for a moment and then looked down the corridor in the direction that they had been heading. It ended roughly forty feet away, at a metal gate. Two Hunters were standing the other side of the gate, watching them. Neither moved to help the old man.

I guess I'm not the only one not used to helping folks, he thought. Then he leaned forward, about to help the man before catching sight of something that made him hesitate.

Blisters and pustules on the man's skin. Bright yellow sores surrounded by red, peeling skin.

Plague, he thought. *That's Ratters Plague.*

Over the years, Jack had seen many types of illnesses. In the Outer Zone there were few people who could heal, and even fewer who were willing. At The Crossing was an apothecary who sold herbs and salves that could help, but for serious illnesses such as Coughing Fever, Sweats, and Ratters Plague, there was no help. You either died from it or you lived.

Most died.

But Ratter's Plague was contagious. And Jack had seen just what it was capable of doing when he was barely twenty-five years old.

THIS OLD TOWN

Many Years Before

Just twenty miles from The Crossing, out near the ruins of the Great Stadium, there had once been a small, growing community. Over the years, Jack had seen it expand from the first few settlers, who struggled to fight off bandits, wild animals, and night creatures, to dozens more who started to build defensive walls. They had a water source there, or so it was said, and had even started to run their own market. Then, one summer, just after the cold weather had abated and Jack had found a particularly good haul of junk, Jack realised he was in that area of the new community and decided to go there to trade instead of travelling further to get to The Crossing or Dartston. Both were roughly equal distance away and would take a whole day, maybe more, to reach. But the new place, which folks were now calling New Stadium, was only a couple of miles away and he realised he could be there before dark. He'd been there a number of times before but only because he had been passing. This time he had a reason to head directly there.

But he'd noticed the change even before he got near the outer wall. It was dusk, and the sun was barely a slither on the horizon, and yet the gates were wide open – a thing unknown with all the dangers lurking outside.

And there were no sentries atop the wall.

Jack remembered standing outside the gates, just ten yards from the wall, and staring at the utterly lifeless street beyond.

"You don't wanna go in there," said a voice from a short distance away. The wind was howling heavily, a stark contrast to the early breeze he had experienced during the day, and he only just heard the warning. Jack had turned to see a stranger – a man – sitting at the side of the road, outside a shop front on the corner of the street just beyond the gates to the new but now seemingly abandoned settlement. He noticed that he man was wearing a cloth around his mouth, and he also noticed that he carried an axe.

Jack had slowly reached to his side, to touch his machete, but the man had seen it.

"I've no bone to pick with you, if you don't wanna go that way."

And Jack hadn't. His hand lingered at the machete for a moment, but then he took it away and started walking over the broken ground to the stranger.

"What happened?" he'd asked as he got closer. He stopped twenty feet away, judging that if the man changed his mind and leapt for him, he'd still have time to draw and be ready.

"Plague," said the man. "Someone in there, guy called Harris, took to ratting just before I last came by here, 'bout two weeks ago. Well, I bin in there just now and seen them. It seems they all done caught themselves a nasty rash."

Jack stood silently for a moment, just staring at the gates.

"Just a rash?"

The man shook his head.

"Much more than a rash."

"Is there no one left in there at all?"

The man nodded.

"Sure," he said, placing his axe on the floor and reaching for a pouch on his belt. He started rolling a cigarette. "Three, maybe four left. They're all infected. So I left them. I asked if they wanted me to, you know, end it, but none of them even recognised that I was there. Only one crazy guy throwing stones. Reckon I should have put them out of their misery, but they

104

didn't answer me, so I couldn't bring myself to do it."

The man finished rolling his smoke, and then, surprisingly, held out the pouch.

"Take one if you want, just go easy on the weed, okay?"

Jack had accepted and a few minutes later the two men were sitting at the side of the road, smoking their cigarettes.

As Jack sat there, slowly smoking the harsh, dry tobacco, his gaze drifted over to the gates once more. He didn't know if it was some form of morbid curiosity, or just a random uncontrollable urge, but he found himself struggling to resist going into the town even with the stranger's warning.

He stood up, nodded at the man and then started to make his way over the road towards the gates.

"You'll regret it," the stranger called after him, but said nothing more. The man must have realised that there was little point trying to stop somebody when their mind was made up, or maybe he just didn't care.

The gates were built from sheets of hammered car body parts, and as Jack approached he could clearly see the outline of several car doors, a roof, and dozens of hood panels, all hammered flat and then secured together with bolts. The wall itself was mostly more cars, turned on their side and propped up by piles of broken up masonry. Even though it had been centuries, there was still an abundance of abandoned vehicles littering the streets if you went far enough out, away from the sealed off city. The people who built this town had laboured for many months to collect the materials for the wall, Jack thought, realising that he had never considered it before. Scrap metal was low on the list of items he searched for when scavenging.

As he passed through the open gates, Jack looked to his left, to where a rusty old caravan was propped up on bricks just a few yards from the gate. The town folk used it as a gatehouse of sorts, and on the few occasions that Jack had visited there had always been a guard or two sitting outside the caravan, watching the entrance. Now the spot was devoid of life, and the door to the caravan was wide open.

He looked down the long street that was the main part of the settlement and saw no one, not a single person moving around. The settlement was quite small, and comprised of one long main street and a few alleyways that had been blocked up. Most of the buildings had their windows boarded up on the outside, and the alleyways were built up with salvaged bricks from other nearby buildings so that the outer buildings along the street also made up part of the defensive wall that surrounded the place on all sides. There were probably twenty houses in total, all facing into the street apart from the few farm buildings at the far end.

As Jack moved towards the first house, he noticed something at the end of the street that hadn't been there the last time he had visited. He walked halfway along the street, stepping over cracks and weeds, but then stopped a hundred yards from what looked like a huge pile of dirt. Next to it was a hole, and even from the distance he was at he could see something that made him think twice about going any further.

The people from the settlement had dug a large hole just a few dozen yards from the farm plot, and there, sticking up from among the weeds and grass, was a foot. From where Jack was, that was all he could see, but his own imagination had told him far more than was visible.

It was a mass grave, just like the ones that had been dug on the outskirts of 342nd Street during the reign of Jagan and his pit slavers.

Jack stopped, took a step back, and was about to leave when he heard a noise to his right. Adrenaline kicked in, and Jack turned quickly, both hands going to the machetes on his belt, ready to draw and fight if need be, cursing himself for not just carrying them ready in the first place. But he didn't draw.

He didn't have to. The man that had made the noise wasn't going anywhere fast.

In front of him was a single-storey building with a porch that was half-missing. Most of the wood had probably been stripped away years ago, to be used as firewood, but some of the decking planks and a section of the railing on the right side of the house was still there. The front door was wide open now, and swung further out as the figure – a man dressed in what appeared to be rags – first leaned on the door frame, and then stumbled out onto the deck to collapse onto a bench that was placed against the front wall.

Jack narrowed his eyes, watching the man intently as he struggled to right himself, one hand fumbling to push himself up. Eventually the man leaned back and gave a rattling sigh, and that gave Jack a better view of his face. He was covered in grey and brown pock marks, and his eyes were swollen and puffy.

"Take whatever you want," said the man, lifting his arm slowly and waving his hand around, indicating the building around them. "Ain't no one needing anything around here no more. All dead."

Jack stood there for a moment, his hands wavering over the hilts of his machetes, but then he took his hands away. There was no threat of violence here. Only the dead or the dying.

"Everyone's dead?"

The man nodded. "Ayuh. Everyone who stayed. Just me alive now, and I'm for the dirt soon, I reckon."

Jack's thoughts zoomed back to the last few times he had been at the settlement. There had been families there and several children, probably fifty people in total, maybe more. He vividly remembered a young girl and boy, both maybe five years old, playing in the street.

"Even the kids?" he asked, not sure if he wanted an answer. He glanced along the road again, at the naked foot sticking up in the air, poking out of the grave. Was that a child's or a woman's? He couldn't tell.

"Nah. They got taken off when the first of us caught the pox. That would be Tall Al and his wife Susan's kids. Al packed up and left and took them all with him. Don't know where they went. But they dint catch it, I'm thinking. I hope so, anyway. Hope they got away before it caught them."

The man coughed loudly, and then the cough turned into a heaving fit, until he leaned over and spat out a glob of grey mucus spotted with blood. Jack grimaced. The man looked up and laughed.

"How about we do a bit of trade here?" the man asked.

Jack frowned and opened his mouth to speak but then stopped. He was puzzled. What the hell could the man want? He was a day at most from dying. If any scavengers wanted to raid the village, they could just walk in and take whatever they wanted.

"A deal. If you can manage."

Jack peered at him warily. "What kind of deal?"

The man coughed again, then he took a few deep breaths, his chest rising rapidly with effort. "Got me a nice weapon back in there, locked up. Single barrel shot and thirty rounds, but the damn thing is in a case and I can't open it. My hands don't wanna work the lock. I gave up trying. Look. If you can take the key and take out the gun, you can have the damn thing."

"And what do you want out of it?" Jack asked.

"An end to this," stated the man.

Three minutes later, Jack walked out of the main gates and glanced over the street to where the stranger had been. He was still sitting there, and as Jack walked across the street towards him, he saw the man's hand reach to his belt, to something metal there.

Jack stopped, and raised his hands. "I still don't want any trouble," he said.

The stranger watched him for a moment, his gaze

jumping from Jack's face to the shotgun in his hand.

"I heard the shot," said the stranger, relaxing once more. "Thought that you must have gone into that crazy fellow's house."

Jack smiled. "You met him already?"

The stranger nodded. "Yeah. I went in there, took a look in a couple of houses and got to his. Damn crazy ass only started throwing rocks at me from his window. Missed, thankfully. He was raving and waving his arms in the air. So I took off. Figured I'd wait him out instead of risking getting smacked on the head."

Jack stopped at the side of the road and looked at the shotgun in his hand.

"And you figured if I went in I might save you the trouble?"

The stranger looked up.

"No. No. I did warn you."

Jack smiled and the stranger smiled back.

"No foul?" the stranger asked.

Jack nodded. "No foul."

"Good," said the stranger.

"I'm Jack."

The stranger grinned. "Drogan," he said. "Pleased to

meet you."

CAUGHT

Drogan.

The thought of his friend from way back then made Jack feel a pang of nostalgia for the days that had passed and times that would never return, but right then, standing in the tunnel, Jack knew he had to do something about the old guy with Ratter's Plague before a lot of other people were dead.

He turned away from the man and started forward, hurrying towards the three Hunters that waited at the gate at the end of the tunnel. As he approached, one of the Hunters turned his head toward Jack, then nodded at the other two and slowly drew his shock-stick. He stood there, the other side of the gate, watching Jack.

Jack slowed as he got to the gate, and then turned and pointed at the old diseased man, who was slowly making his way down the tunnel. Behind the man, Jack could see several other captives in the tunnel, and a few of them were catching up to the old man.

If any tried to help him, Jack thought, *if anyone touches the guy, they're as good as dead.*

"That man," said Jack, talking to the Hunter that had drawn the shock-stick. "That old guy has a disease."

"Move through," Jack heard. The voice was metallic and emotionless. He turned back and saw that the Hunters had opened the gate and were stepping aside. The one with the shock-stick drawn flicked the glowing bat, indicating that Jack should go through.

"But the guy," said Jack, turning back again.

"Move through, immediately," said the voice. Again it was emotionless and flat. Jack turned back to the Hunters and glanced at each of them in turn, realising that they weren't even listening to him, and started forward, moving between the three armoured figures and out into the room beyond. He glanced back and saw that the nearest captive behind the old man caught up, glanced briefly at him, and moved on, walking past and away from the old guy.

He sighed. *It's not even in people's nature to consider helping when it could save them too*, he thought. He turned back, looking into the room ahead. *I would have done the same a few years ag*o, he thought.

Before you met the boy. That was how things were. You would never have stopped to help the man. But he couldn't help but feel a little resentful towards both the man who had just passed the stricken old fellow and the Hunters at the gate. Emotionless, all of them. *Just like you were, once. If you hadn't met the boy, and hadn't learned to care, would you have just walked by the old man? After all, that is what you did anyway. You didn't try to help him. But he's diseased. You could have caught it, and then where would you be? You'd be exactly where the old guy will be a week from now. Dying, or already dead, or bleeding from everywhere, just like the man on the porch had been. Bleeding out of your nose, and your eyes, and your ears.*

Jack closed his eyes and tried to force the feelings of guilt to pass. *You killed him. With his own shotgun. But he had asked you to do it. Yes, he had asked, but you didn't even hesitate. But that was before. Before. Everything changed with Ryan.*

And anyway, it was merciful, wasn't it?

Ahead of him was a platform of some kind, maybe thirty yards long, with a metal rail along the edge. Beyond that he saw a row of windows lining something that was painted a bright white. He recognised it from somewhere, and tried to think how.

A picture you've seen? But when? What was it?

In the middle of the platform was another booth, just like the ones in the huge chamber where people were being... sorted. *That was what they had been doing,* Jack thought. *They were sorting us. But this one wasn't. This was different.*

A group of three more Hunters stood at the booth on the edge of the platform. One was next to what looked like a metal seat that had wheels on the bottom. Beyond that was a door-shaped opening in the wall of windows.

Jack walked forward and stopped at the booth. The first Hunter indicated the seat, and Jack complied, wondering what was coming next. He had just noticed that all of the windows on the wall next to the booth were blacked out when he felt a sharp, stabbing pain in his shoulder. He looked down, staring at the spot where the pain had erupted, and saw another of the Hunters withdrawing a needle of some kind.

It's just like the pain from the dart. The one that Jagan's slavers shot you with.

A wave of dizziness swept over him and he felt his feet begin to tingle. The tingling sensation spread rapidly along his legs, up his body and into his arms, then his neck and his face. As it flooded over his cheeks Jack felt the world slipping away.

Will they put you in a fighting pit? he thought.

No. He didn't think so.

THE PIT

Many Years Before

Jack threw his weight to his left, hit the floor and rolled. Behind him, he heard a sharp clang as something hit the ground, hard. He pushed himself up, jumping to his feet, and spun around, instinctively swinging the wooden bat in his hand around in an arc as he came up. But his opponent wasn't there. Instead, the man was away across the other side of the pit, hopping from foot to foot, almost dancing as he swung the flail around his head.

The crowd above roared their enthusiasm, and Jack made the mistake of glancing up. Above him, maybe fifteen feet from the floor of the pit, was a metal railing attached to a barbed-wire fence, and looking down at him were dozens of faces, all of them wide-eyed, many of them grinning. A cacophony of voices assaulted his senses as the crowd shouted words that he couldn't decipher.

And it was a mistake to take his eyes off his opponent. Jack felt, more than saw, the man rush forward, and he sensed the flail – a ball of stone attached to a handle by a long chain, swing towards his head. He threw himself sideways again, rolling away, as a rush of wind brushed past him.

"Oh! It looks like we found a lively one!" came a booming voice, seemingly from all around him. But Jack was too busy avoiding the man with the flail to locate the speakers that the voice bellowed out from.

He gripped his bat too tight, his fingers turning white from the exertion, and once again threw himself away from his opponent, coming up across the pit again.

This time the man facing him stood still for a moment, his head cocked to one side as he scrutinised Jack.

He's weighing you up, Jack thought. *He's looking for a weakness. Well, he shouldn't have much trouble. There are enough of them.*

The fight was obviously unfair and intentionally so. Jack had heard of the pit fights, and how those that were part of Jagan's clan used them as entertainment, and he knew that he was meant to die there. His opponent was armed with a more lethal weapon, and wearing a leather jacket and leather trousers, but he was also wearing a motorcycle helmet with a mask attached, and some shoulder pads made of a material that Jack didn't recognise. Was it metal? Reinforced plastic? A lot of Jagan's men wore armour scavenged from the ruins or made from scrap metal. Jack, on the other hand, was wearing what he had left when they brought him in, just the t-shirt and a pair of ripped jeans.

Jack stood there, breathing heavily, as the man started to circle around, edging towards him, and still swinging the flail.

One hit from that thing and it will all be over, he thought, also considering his own weapon. It was a wooden bat, and thin. If he tried to use it to hit the man over the head, against the motorcycle helmet, he might dent the helmet, even stun the man, but the bat would most likely break. It already had some cracks in it.

And then the choice was taken away from him as the man lurched forward, jumping the distance between them and swinging the heavy stone ball down towards his head. Jack stumbled, falling backwards, but still he tried to bring the bat up, tried to defend himself. He felt the wind rush out of his chest as he hit the floor, and then felt a jolt in his arm followed by the sound of wood cracking. He rolled sideways, and only just in time as the heavy stone flail came swinging in for a second strike. Again it missed him by inches and bounced off the floor where he had been just a moment before.

Jack pulled back the bat, about to attempt a strike, when he saw that half of the weapon was lying on the floor a few feet away. All that was left in his hand was a foot-long splinter attached to the rubber grip.

His opponent came on again, swinging the flail around his head, and all Jack could do was back away towards the wall. His shoulder hit wood and he realised, with certainty, that he had gone as far as he could. The next lunge would be his end.

And then it came. The man stepped forward and swung the flail low, coming in from the side, and faster than he'd expected, but Jack, unarmoured as he was, was faster. He fell sideways and felt the heavy stone of the flail hit the wall. And then the man's eyes went wide as the ball smashed through the wooden barrier and stuck there. Jack's opponent had just half a second to attempt to pull the flail out from the wall, and he heaved on it, wood splintering and cracking, but the flail didn't move. It was stuck fast in the dirt behind the barrier, and Jack saw his moment. Just as the man let go of the flail, and reached for the knife at his side, Jack lunged forward and rammed the sharp end of his broken bat at the man's neck.

Luck, it seemed, was with him. The wood splinter burst through the leather around the man's neck and into his throat. Jack pushed hard, but then let go of the bat, his hands jarring with the impact, as he stumbled back and fell to the floor.

He gasped for breath, heard the crowd above the pit roaring with enthusiasm, and watched as his opponent grabbed hold of the bat and stumbled. Blood poured down the man's chest and down his arms.

"We have a winner!" came the bellowing sound of the match's commentator. The crowd above roared.

"Bring him on up!"

But the world around Jack darkened and span, and he fell forward into the dirt. He was vaguely aware of boots on the ground around him for a moment, but then he passed out.

That had been the first fight, but not his last.

CAUGHT

The darkness of unconsciousness after the fight felt much the same as what Jack now experienced. Except this time, as the world came back in a swirling lack of colour, he wasn't lying on the floor of a cage, but on a metal bed attached to the wall of a chamber even smaller than the cage he had spent most of his time in down in The Pits. But the walls of this new prison were solid, grey metal, and the only light came from a circular disc in the ceiling.

It took him a while to sit up, and he rubbed his forehead, trying to alleviate the throb of the headache that now pounded on the inside of his skull.

How long have you been out? An hour? A day? It could be any amount of time and you wouldn't know.

At least the cage in The Pits had a view of daylight.

There was something else. Something, as he sat there on the bed, looking around at the room that was void of any furniture apart from the bed, that bothered him. His stomach was churning and his head felt light.

Motion, he thought. *It's motion sickness. That's what I'm feeling. I'm moving. Or rather, the chamber that I'm in is moving.*

A Trans.

That was what the windows had reminded him of.

The picture that he had once found of the strange, amazing construction that had been created by the people of long ago, and used, somehow, to travel great distances. The magazine from the bottom of the dumpster in the old factory north of The Crossing and out towards the Ashlands. It had a picture of such a thing, and a long story about something called a Trans. That was what had been next to the booth in the last hall, and what he had seen before they made him sit in the wheeled chair and injected him.

I'm on a Trans.

But where am I going?

PROMOTION DEMOTION

Lisa sat looking at the window of the Trans carriage. Outside, a beautiful sunset raged over the forested hills. A deep orange glow, sliced with yellow and red, covered most of the landscape and highlighted the endless sea of spruce trees that covered the land. Except none of those trees were alive and Lisa knew it. Even if the land above had once been covered with trees, it would be difficult to look at them through the window she faced.

The Trans hummed along the track, barely making an audible sound as it swept along. It was nearly two hundred feet underground, rather than up on the surface, and the dazzling view of sunset was actually a screen display to make the enclosure of the carriage less stifling.

Lisa looked away from the screen and back down to the display pad in her hands. There, in bold type, were her new orders and her new assignment. She sighed heavily and closed her eyes for a moment before continuing to read.

The last few hours had been the worst of her career so far. That something could change so quickly, and for a misdemeanour that she considered so small, was beyond her. And yet, she thought back to the meeting that she had been called to attend with the Section Governor, a big, bearded man called Alderton, and she realised that it was only she that thought it minor.

"So, Corporal...Markell. You were reported for removing your faceguard while out on duty. Do you have anything to say on the matter?" the tall man had said, and Lisa could tell that he was not impressed, and that he wouldn't treat the incident lightly. But even so, she hadn't expected it to go as far as it had.

"Your record is exemplary. Top performance, high discipline record. Excellent. Not so high a delivery record in the last couple of months. Hmm...not so good, but that's common at the moment, so we can overlook that."

Alderton hadn't offered her the chance to reply and had merely continued to rattle on.

"We can't ignore the misdemeanour of removing your face guard, though. I have been advised to use the highest discipline in accordance, but I'm not an unreasonable man, and considering your record, I think the best choice will be to reassign you to a new duty. Take you off the recruitment operation. The alternative is to discharge you, and I'm sure neither of us wants that."

And apart from some formalities, that had been it. After two minutes of listening to Alderton, she had been dismissed and told to go and wait in her quarters for her new assignment.

That had been just two hours ago, and her new assignment was waiting for her on the system when she got back to the barracks, with instructions to be packed up and waiting at the Trans terminal in twenty-five minutes.

Twenty-five minutes. That was all they had given her. And the rest of her squad were out of the barracks and on duty, not to return for at least six more hours. She didn't even get to say goodbye to them. Instead, she had quickly packed her few personal belongings and hurried out of her room, heading to the terminal and arriving with just five minutes to spare.

Guard duties at the NE7 Resource Recycling Facility.

She'd heard of the place before. It was where they sent a huge number of captives after they were sorted into possible abilities at the terminal. In fact, Lisa knew that on the very Trans she was on, there would be fifty or more new workers heading for that very facility.

Resource Recycling Facility. That was a joke. The place was a rubbish dump, far, far out into the

126

Ashlands across the dead waters. It was a place that killed most of the workers sent to work there. There were stories from many years before, from a long time before Lisa was born, that said the NE7 zone was used as a rubbish tip for the city, a place so far away that it wouldn't matter what they dumped there. And yet it was now used as a salvage area, where captured workers would sift through the rubbish to find anything of use.

A promotion, the assignment had been called in her note from Alderton. She was now promoted to First Corporal, and would be in charge of expedition security.

And what the hell was that anyway? Expeditionary? It was a damn demotion was what it was, she thought. Bastard *decided to get rid of me, send me out into the far away, into the ashes. And probably only because firing a trooper was not the done thing.*

Lisa sighed again and wondered what her parents would think when they found out, or her brothers. Her position and pay were the mainstay of her family's tickets on the next transport off-world. She hoped to hell this wouldn't damage their chances.

Her thoughts were snapped back to the Trans as a light went on at the far end of the carriage, followed by a repetitive buzzing noise that grated at her nerves. She had been alone in the large, spacious compartment for over two hours, for most of the journey, but now the far doors hissed open and two Trans staff stepped swiftly into the room and sat down in the nearest seats.

"All passengers please be seated for deceleration," came a metallic voice from the speakers above her head. The voice echoed somehow, or maybe it was just her imagination. The message repeated a dozen times and then stopped. Then there was a loud sound of rushing air from all around her. Lisa felt her stomach lurching, as though it didn't want to stay where the rest of her was.

The display panel to her left switched off for a few seconds, the beautiful forest scene vanishing from view, and Lisa felt a strange pang of regret. But there was no time for her to mourn the loss of a fake scene, for the screen flickered – as did the others in the carriage – and then an image of a very different place appeared, this one very real.

And First Corporal Lisa Markell got her first glimpse of a place that she wished she'd had never had to visit.

CAUGHT

Jack forced his hands up to the wall, trying to prop himself up as the Trans began to slow down. There had been no warning. One moment he had been sitting in the middle of the room, staring at the blank wall, and the next his stomach had heaved and he slid across the polished floor to bump into the wall. Realising that raising his arms to sit himself up was only going to make him feel worse, he lay flat on the ground and waited for the motion sickness to abate.

Had Ryan laid on the cold metal floor when he travelled here? If he travelled here. That had bothered Jack from the moment he'd watched the huge man being dragged off to the Conversion Facility, to a different place. And then the sorting of people, and the different corridors that led to...wherever they all led. He'd presumed that all captives went to the same place. But the possibility that he would be sent somewhere completely different had become very real.

But maybe he was wrong to think so, maybe Ryan had sat in the very same chamber, wondering where he was going. Jack lifted his hand and traced the outline of a stick-man and then a smaller stick-man next to it.

All you managed to get the boy for his birthday was a pair of crayons. Sure, they were colours he didn't have, but it wasn't much, was it? Had Ryan sat here and drawn his stick-men on these walls?

It was foolish to think that, of course. He knew that. Whatever reasons the Hunters captured people, they would be different for each person, surely? Grown adults who were healthy would be sent to work somewhere, and the sick would be...well...he didn't know where they would go.

He estimated that it took two minutes for the Trans to stop. Jack had presumed that the other corridor, where the limping man and the old woman had gone, would lead to the place where they dealt with that, but he'd been sent down the same damn corridor as a man sick with Ratter's Plague. As for children, they would surely go somewhere else.

Jack sighed and tried not to dry heave, but his stomach wrenched with spasms as the motion of the slowing Trans reached its most violent. For a moment, he thought that he would actually be sick, or maybe pass out, but then the feeling was gone. The Trans had stopped.

He lay there for a few seconds, his head spinning, before taking a deep breath and sitting up. His stomach growled loudly enough for him to hear it.

How long is it since you ate, anyway? Three days at least. Has to be. The wheat bread you traded for with those nails, wasn't it? Damn that stuff had tasted nasty. And that had to be three days, unless you've been out cold for longer.

And how fast had the Trans been travelling for it to take so long to stop?

Stupidly fast.

Jack sighed, and sat there in the dim light, wondering how long he would have to wait before the door opened and they ushered him off to somewhere else.

Almost as though someone was listening to his thoughts, the door at the other end of the tiny compartment hissed open and a green light flickered on above it. Jack hadn't noticed the tiny panel above the door frame and cursed himself for it.

Years ago you would have spotted something like that. But he wasn't given long enough to properly berate himself before a metallic voice spoke from the panel.

"Immediately exit the compartment and turn right."

Jack frowned.

No guards?

He waited a moment, wondering just what would happen if he sat there and ignored the voice.

"Immediately exit the compartment and turn right," repeated the voice, and as Jack watched, one of the other captives shuffled past the doorway. The man looked confused and more than a little dazed.

Pretty much how you feel.

Jack rose to his feet, deciding that he wasn't really so keen on finding out what would happen if he didn't do as the voice said, and then started to walk towards the door. The old man passing by the door glanced at him.

I know him. That's the guy with Ratter's Plague.

Jack stopped, watching the man from the middle of the room. He'd expected to never see the guy again, expected them to cart him off to somewhere, wherever they dealt with nasty diseased people.

Probably a pit.

But then he noticed that the man's skin was no longer mottled with red pock marks.

Jack frowned, and looked the man in the eyes.

"I'm not sick no more," said the old man, raising his hands to look at them, his expression that of a child seeing something unknown for the first time. Then he touched his chest. "It don't hurt here no more," he said, a grin spreading across his grizzled and scarred face.

"Immediately exit the compartment and turn right," repeated the metallic voice, but this time it continued. "Ten seconds to purge."

Purge? What the hell is purge? That does not sound good.

Jack hurried forward. Ratter's Plague or not, purge sounded a lot worse. He stepped out of the room and stood next to the old man, who although apparently clear of the nasty blotches that came with the disease, still stank like a three-week-dead dog.

The corridor was filled with people now, a few of whom Jack recognised from their brief gathering in the landing area, and as he looked up and down the corridor he saw dozens of open doors spaced a few feet apart.

Then he heard the protests.

"I'm not going anywhere!"

Whoever the man was, he was a few doors up from Jack's compartment, and on the other side of the carriage. In front of the door, a woman stood frowning at the open door.

"Get out of there, you idiot," she said, and gestured to the space in front of her.

"Five seconds to purge," said the metallic voice.

"I said...I'm not going anywhere."

The woman looked around at the other captives, and then back at the door. No one responded, and Jack could see that she was hesitating.

Was she actually considering going in there after the guy? He hoped not.

And she didn't, but she wasn't giving up. "Don't be a fool. Get out of there."

But it was too late.

"Purge commencing," said the metallic voice. And in response, every door along the corridor hissed closed.

"What the hell kinda joke is this anyway?" came the muffled voice of the man now trapped in his compartment.

A second hissing sound filled the corridor, but Jack didn't see any doors opening. What he did see was a thin wisp of smoke, or steam, coming from under the doorway of the room that he had just left.

There was a short, loud scream from the compartment with the man trapped in it, but that was cut off barely half a second later, and then silence. The captives looked round at each other, none of them – including Jack – knowing what to say. All of them terrified.

No kinda joke is what this is.

Light flooded the corridor, and the sound of more doors hissing open, and the metallic voice was speaking again, urging everyone to exit the Trans through the open doors.

A Trans. That's what it was called.

Jack trundled along with the others, not sure if he was looking forward to being back outside or if he was dreading what he would see there.

This is the place they take them to. This is where it starts. If they brought Ryan here, then this is where you get to begin looking for him.

Jack stepped out of the Trans and headed down a long ramp, his eyes fighting to adjust to the bright glow of daylight, straining to focus on his surroundings. And when he finally did, he wondered if he would have been better off just staying in his compartment and dying like the other fool.

END OF THE EARTH

Lisa stood on the platform, almost oblivious to the crowd of people being ushered from the prison compartments just twenty yards away, and stared, drop-jawed, at what was in front of her.

The facility itself was probably a square mile in size, and the Trans station rose from the ground, higher up than the rest of the facility by maybe fifty feet, an elevation that was enough to see beyond the outer walls. Because it wasn't the rows of prefab buildings that caught her attention. They were common enough in the work facilities across The City and she had seen enough of those in military camps before, including the camps outside of the barrier wall.

It also wasn't the massive warehouses on the far side of the facility, though she hadn't expected to see anything quite so big out here. She knew she was being posted out in the middle of nowhere, but the Outer Zone was as far as she had ever gone, and the sprawl of ruins outside of the barrier was familiar to her now, but this place was something almost alien.

Outside of the perimeter fence, which was a thirty foot high wall with solid concrete towers and barbed wire that looked like it was maybe three separate fences rather than just one, was an endless mass of junk.

An endless mass that went on and on to the very horizon.

Instead of rolling, burned grey hills, like she had seen at the edge of the Ashlands, this landscape was made of trash. Ruined buildings stuck up from the junk here and there, dotting the landscape every few miles like broken teeth inside a rotten mouth, but they were few and scattered randomly.

This was where she had been posted. To watch over mountains of trash.

The histories and rumours that she had heard had been right. It had to have been a dumping ground of some kind, maybe centuries back, but how was there so much of it? This wasn't just a few square miles of junk. No, this was endless miles of it, and most of it looked like it had just been dropped from a great height to fall in piles that now sculpted the hills on the landscape.

As she stood watching, she became aware of movement around her. Troopers were forcefully guiding prisoners from the other compartments near the back of the Trans and pushing them in droves down the slope towards the first building, a hundred yards across the dusty ground.

And then she noticed a single figure nearby, on the edge of the crowd. The man wasn't moving. Instead he stood looking out at the junk landscape with an expression of hopelessness.

And she recognised him.

It was him. The man she had picked up just hours before. The damn fool that had walked up to the back of her truck and spoken to her. The one she had lifted her helmet to reply to, cursing herself to be sent out here in the process.

He was here with her.

Both of them sentenced to live at the end of the Earth.

JUNK

Six Months Later…

"Avery!" called an impatient voice.

Most of the workers ignored the tall, stocky trooper dressed in grey, ablative armour as he paced across the dirty floor of the warehouse. They were all too busy keeping their heads down and hoping to be ignored, and busy sifting through the massive piles of junk that littered the huge open space, sorting out the recyclable bits from the trash that needed to be thrown away.

And there was a lot of it to wade through. The warehouse was the biggest building in the NE7 Resource Recycling Facility, and easily stood seventy feet high and several hundred feet across in both directions, and it was probably the only original structure that was still standing. If *standing* was what you could call it. Every fifty feet or so a thick stone pillar jutted up from the floor, and they certainly weren't part of the old building, but constructed to stop the rusted and cracked roof from collapsing in on everyone.

The rest of the buildings in the two square mile

Recycling Facility were prefabricated, and looked a lot newer, even if they were just as dirty. The original settlement teams had salvaged what they could of the surrounding buildings, but most of them had been smashed into the ground and new prefabs brought in and built on-site. Most of those were enclosed, and some even had air conditioning, but the Goods In building was open to the elements and the polluted air.

The thousands of square metres of cracked concrete ground inside the Goods In building were overflowing with piles of junk delivered from the transport dock at the other end of the building – where the dumpers that made the journey out to the salvager camps each day would deliver whatever they had recovered. There were ten delivery bays and every evening, just as the sun was setting, the trucks would come roaring through the gate, pull up at the back of their designated bay, and unceremoniously drop their contents onto the ground. The next morning, new piles of scrap greeted the weary workers of the sorting crews.

The guard paced around a pile of rubber tyres, glared at the worker hauling another tyre over to the pile, and called out a second time.

"Avery! Where the hell are you?"

The worker dropped the tyre on the pile and pointed the far end of the warehouse. The trooper glanced in the direction that the worker indicated, seeing only darkness in the corner and piles upon piles of scrap. He frowned, but started over towards the corner. As he rounded a particularly large pile of scrap metal, he spotted a man hunched over what appeared to be a trolley of some kind.

"Avery," he said, the irritation in his voice obvious.

The man stopped what he was doing, turned, and stood up, scratching his head. The trooper grinned as he noticed the man's expression turn from one of puzzlement to that of nervousness. He could almost smell the fear and he thought that was good.

Let the scum be frightened, the trooper thought. *He'll be more frightened soon. Look at him. He's a wretch anyway, covered in dirt and crap like the rest of them.*

"You Avery?" asked the trooper, glancing down at the card in his hand that bore the man's name and designation.

Jack nodded. "Yes...yes, sir," he stuttered, wondering what the hell one of the guards wanted with him. He'd learned a lot in the last few months that he had been a worker at the Recycling Facility, and one of the most important things was to remain unnoticed, to just get on with what you had to do, and keep out from under the eyes of the guards. People who drew attention tended to disappear and not re-appear.

"Got your re-assignment card here," said the trooper, holding out the card.

Jack felt a further twinge of fear creep up his back. Re-assignment. That wasn't good. Where he was, in the sorting plant, he was relatively safe. The area was radiation free – well, low radiation anyway – and he was fed and had a place to sleep. It wasn't the easiest of jobs, hauling the scrap that came back from the expeditions each day, it was hard work, and he often went to bed at night exhausted beyond that which a normal man could cope with. But at least he wasn't gradually rotting from poisoning, or out in The Junklands, avoiding a million deadly insects and vermin.

"We have a new vacancy on the north side salvage expeditionary, and lucky you, your number came up."

The guard stepped forward, stuffed the card into Jack's hand, and turned to leave, but he stopped a few feet away and turned back, grinning. Jack thought there was zero friendliness in that smile.

"Report to the bay in five minutes. They leave soon, and if you aren't on the truck you can follow them on foot. You'll need to pack down your gear from your bunk and take it with you. No sleeping in the main compound for you anymore. Good luck with the scabs," said the trooper, and then turned and walked away, leaving Jack staring down at a card that he suspected might be a death sentence.

He'd seen the condition of most of the scabs. They were the ones who went out on the trucks each week, the ones whose job it was to search among the mountains of trash and debris outside of the facility, trash that had been dumped there over centuries by not only the protected central city, but the cities and people that lived even before the world started dying. The scabs were tasked with bringing back resources, which meant salvage, and because of that they spent most of their time outside of the facility, out in the wastes where radiation could easily spike up and be unnoticed until, well, until it was too late to do anything about it. They were mostly quite sick individuals, covered in scabs, scars and burns, with their hair and teeth quite often falling out. He been told many times by other workers that when the scabs died, the body would be left out in The Junklands, discarded to rot wherever the poor individual fell, and then someone from elsewhere in the facility would be required to replace them.

No one wanted to be a replacement, but there had been at least twenty replacements made in the six months that Jack had been at the facility, and he was also convinced that some of those who replaced the fallen had also gone on to die of sickness.

He rubbed some of the oil from his hands onto his tatty jeans, glanced at the trolley full of machine parts salvaged the day before, and thought of the drying blood he'd found on one of the parts. It had sharp edges, and looked like some sort of blade for a large machine. Whoever had salvaged it had cut themselves, maybe. Was that the drying blood of his predecessor?

Five minutes was all he had, and he had to go fetch his stuff from his bunk or lose it. He headed across the warehouse, towards the western entrance to the sleeping compound. He could see the guard already exiting the warehouse at the other end and followed.

As he walked across the building, he tried not to take notice of the glances that were cast in his direction by the other workers. He knew they all meant well. They felt sorry for him but were thankful at the same time. If he was going, they were off the hook for maybe one more week before another scab died. He'd felt the same. He tried not to think about it and just kept his head up and walked quickly across the open ground.

Jack squinted in the bright sunlight as he stepped out of Goods In and onto the roadway that led around the perimeter of the facility. Across the dirt track was the compound, and he made his way there, stepping around the deeper puddles.

Two minutes later he stepped back out into the light with his sack over his shoulder. It was every possession he still had, though most of what he'd carried with him when he originally surrendered to the Hunters six months ago had been taken away from him, and he knew he wouldn't see any of it ever again.

Breathing heavily, he took off at a jog towards the expedition building, which was three hundred yards along the dirt track, past the repair centre. *Now that would have been the job to get*, he thought as he passed the repair centre. The workers in the mechanical department were treated far better than anyone else, and Jack had heard that they even had their own rooms. But, of course, the workers in there, as few of them as there were, were highly skilled, and were able to fix just about any problem with vehicles or machines, and they were also responsible for the upkeep of the entire facility's electricity and water, even the air conditioning in the admin building and the troop barracks. Meaning that the troopers and admin needed them.

Scabs, of course, were treated like what they were — dead men walking.

Five minutes, he thought, *probably about two now. And if*

you don't get your ass over there they'll make you walk the road.
And that was basically sending you out to die.
Everyone knew from talking to the scabs that the
trucks travelled ten, twenty or more miles out of the
facility each time, and there was no knowing exactly
where they were going until the truck stopped. If he
didn't make it, and the guards made him go on
foot…well, he didn't want to think about it. He picked
up pace, jogging along the centre of the roadway, and
arrived at the expedition compound just as the garage
doors of the truck bays were opening.

Six months before, when Jack had stepped off the
train and out into the open air of The Junklands, he'd
been horrified at the sight. Even the Outer Zone of the
city had looked more inviting than the tall, fume-
spewing towers that lined the horizon, the sprawl of
dirty buildings, and the lines of workers moving to and
fro. It had looked like a slave camp, and effectively that
was what it was. One of many slave camps in the
Salvage Zone. All of those tall, filth-spitting towers
were processing plants of some kind, or power stations,
or other machine facilities. Everything that the city
didn't want happening near them was out here, manned
by armed troopers and worked by kidnapped Outer
Zone prisoners. Back in the Outer Zone, no one knew
where they took people, and that was because it was
thousands of miles away, in a place that no one from

the Outer Zone could ever get to, and no one was coming back. Not even when they died.

They're better off not knowing, Jack thought.

Now he ignored all the sights and ignored the fact that the sky was dark and filled with fumes. It wasn't worth the worry. He was alive, at least for now. And he hadn't seen a single sign of Ryan in the six months he'd been at the facility, so maybe that was a good thing. That was what Jack told himself. Maybe being sent out of the place was a good thing.

Jack approached the compound, watching the garage doors open and the trucks being driven out onto the gravel courtyard. A group of four troopers came out of the small office next to the building, and Jack turned and headed in their direction. As Jack got closer, one of them stepped forward and held up his hand.

"Identify yourself," she said, her voice slightly muffled. Unlike the Hunters that had stalked the Outer Zone, the troopers in the Recycling Facility didn't wear full helmets that covered their faces. Instead, they wore breathing masks. This meant that you could see their faces, and even after six months Jack still struggled to get used to it.

"Jack Avery," mumbled Jack. "I've been re-assigned."

The guard lifted her hand to her ear, tapped something on the side of her communicator, spoke a few words, waited, and then stepped towards Jack.

"Arms out straight. I have to check you," she said, waiting for him to comply. Jack did as he was told, and stood there, bemused, as the guard took a small device from her utility belt, switched it on and started to move the gadget over his chest and down his arms. The device bleeped when it reached his waist.

"What is that?" the guard asked.

Jack frowned, and then looked down. "Oh," he said, and then unclipped a small wrench from his belt, holding it out. "Just tools."

"Take it off and dump it in your sack," said the guard.

When he had dropped the belt to the floor the guard nodded at him.

"You got your assignment card?" she asked, her expression impatient. As he stood there, searching his pockets for the card he had been given, he thought for a moment that the trooper was sizing him up somehow.

Jack held out the card and the woman took it, glanced at it, and then turned to the trooper standing next to her. He was a tall man, easily half a head above

Jack, and he had to stoop down to peer at the card. The man read the details, then glanced at Jack, his eyes squinting.

"They take these goddamn photos and then expect us to recognise these people after months in the dirt," he scoffed. "Yeah, sure, he'll do."

The female trooper grinned behind her breathing mask.

"Go into the compound, through the main doors, then turn left. Find room E2, that's your new assignment group," she said. "There's an empty bunk in there. Dump your stuff and get straight out here. We're leaving in fifteen minutes, and I presume you know what happens if you're not on the truck when we go?"

"A long walk," said Jack, nodding.

"A very long walk," she said, then she saw how he was frowning and must have read his expression. "Your stuff will still be here when you come back," she said. "Now get."

Room E2 was smaller than he had imagined, containing only six sleeping cots, five of which were ruffled and looked slept in. The sixth, right at the back of the room, was stripped of bedding, and even missing a pillow. Jack presumed that this was his, and dumped his sack on the empty frame and glanced around the room. There was a lot more stuff in there than the sleeping compound at the warehouse. Boxes and cases were piled up in corners, all of them shut, and bags of various sizes were stuffed underneath the cots.

These guys get to keep stuff, he thought, and he considered this unusual, considering how little the workers that slept in the main compound were allowed to own.

The room smelt like wet dog and was warmer than Jack expected. There was a window at the far end – furthest from his cot, he noticed – and several air vents in the ceiling, again something more than what he was used to. There was also a large metal box in the middle of the room with what looked like half of a door lying on top of it. The surface of the makeshift table was littered with empty cans and bottles, and a deck of cards that looked well used. Half a dozen crates surrounded the table.

I don't have time for this, he thought, and turned to leave, ignoring his natural instinct to investigate. He was curious about the contents of every box and bag in the room, and wondered why his bunk was completely bare. The dead man, or woman, must have had possessions, surely. They would in the least have had some bedding.

He hurried out of the room, shutting the door behind him, and headed back out into the courtyard where the carriers stood. The engines were humming now, and dozens of scabs were jumping into the backs of the vehicles through the open doors. He glanced around, wondering which of the dozen or so trucks was the one he should be on, and then saw the female trooper standing a few carriers away, beckoning him towards her.

Jack hurried over, moving between the hurried lines of people jumping into the trucks.

"Get in and buckle up," shouted the trooper, her voice barely audible over the roar of engine. Jack heard the slamming of heavy metal doors as the trucks were closed up, locking in their passengers.

He stepped forward, grabbed the overhead bar just inside the back of the truck, and squinted in the dim light. As he stepped up and into the back of the truck, he heard a creak and a bang as the doors behind him slammed shut. The engine roared even louder, and Jack's heart jumped a beat as he tried to find an empty seat.

"Over here," a voice said, cutting through the noise of the engine, and as Jack's eyes adjusted to the lack of light, he saw five faces looking back at him, and there, just to his left, an empty seat. He stepped forward, turned, and plopped down into the seat just as the truck lurched forward, almost throwing him onto the floor, but he managed to grab hold of the seat as the truck started to move away, his hands searching around him for the safety belt. He thought he could hear laughter from nearby, but ignored it.

"The buckle's near your head, you eejit," said a voice, this one different from the first. Jack reached up and found the belt, and feeling a little stupid, he pulled it down and snapped it into place.

Then he breathed a sigh of relief.

"Well," said a voice next to him. "Talk about a dramatic entrance."

There was more laughter, this time from multiple directions.

"You certainly cut that a bit fine," said another voice, this one right next to him. It was deeper than the other voices.

Jack looked around, and found that his eyes had begun to adjust to the light. There were no windows in the compartment, just a trio of dim, blue lights at the front, and they cast a cold light across the faces that he now saw watching him from the darkness.

Sitting to his right was a very large man, with dark skin and long, dirty, plaited hair that Jack recalled were called dreadlocks. He wasn't sure where he had heard the term, maybe it was something Drogan had said. The man had a burn scar across one side of his face, and Jack could see that one eye was covered with a small patch made of some kind of plastic.

Directly across from Jack was a much older, frailer man, who Jack thought wouldn't have even been as tall as his own shoulders. The man also had long hair, but his was grey, almost white in places, and he had a beard that almost reached his waist. The man was grinning at him, and Jack could see that he had just four teeth, two on top, and two on the bottom, and the humour in that grin made Jack smile.

There were three others in the back of the truck. A heavy-set man of about Jack's age, or so he thought, who wore a furry hat with long flaps that covered his ears and looked as though it was meant for winter rather than the heat of the Salvage Zone. Another man was entirely bald, with piercing grey eyes and thin, almost chiselled features, and lastly, a man with the strangest face that Jack had ever seen. Everything about the man was disproportioned in so many ways. One of his eyes seemed larger than the other, his bent and crooked nose sat too low down on his face, and his chin appeared to be wider than his forehead.

"So, what's your name?" asked the dark-skinned

man with the dreadlocks.

Jack was quiet for a moment, still considering his new companions, and presuming that these were the men that he would be sharing a room with.

"I'm Jack," he said.

The dreadlocked man nodded and smiled. "I'm Tyler," he said. "This fellow over from you is Higgins, the oldest damn scab alive." At that several of the men laughed.

"Old as the junk around us," said the man wearing the winter hat.

"You can laugh," said the bearded old man, "But I'll be here when you're all gone, and who will be laughing when I get divvies on your gear?"

That brought even more laughter.

"Fellow over there," Tyler indicated the man with the winter hat, "is Locks, and not because he has fine hair."

"Nothing wrong with my hair," said Locks.

"Apart from you ain't got much of it under that damn hat," said Higgins. The old man started to chuckle to himself.

"That over there is Rick," Tyler said, indicating the gaunt, hairless man at the far end of the cabin. "He's our watchman. And, lastly, that's Boots over there. And don't mind that he looks like he's been smacked around more times than a pit fighter."

"Meet ya," said Boots, twitching his head to one side several times then, almost immediately, his head fell forward and he fell fast asleep.

"He does that a lot," said Tyler, sighing loudly. "Damage to the brain. So. Seems like you'll be joining our little band of freaks. At least for a while."

Jack frowned. "A while?"

Tyler laughed. "Well, we'll see if you can last it out salvaging. Not everyone can."

Jack was silent for a moment, while he tried to take it all in.

"What happens to those who don't?"

Tyler's cheerful expression turned cold, the smile gone in an instant. "They become a vacancy," he said, then the grin was back, and he burst into laughter.

Jack sighed, feeling a little out of his depth among these new people. He had not been outside of the facility in the entire six months since he stepped from the transport, and had no idea what to expect. All he had seen so far was the rolling hills of junk and the smog-producing towers in the distance. Now he was in the back of a truck with five strangers, heading out of the facility and miles into The Junklands.

He looked around at the other men.

Strangers.

Strange was certainly the key here.

A VIEW FROM THE TOP

A Week Before

First Corporal Lisa Markell blinked in the bright sunlight and looked back through the viewfinder. From the platform on top of the armoured carrier, perched high upon a mound of debris and junk, she could see for miles. Not that it gave her much of an advantage.

She could see even more trash, and that was about it. Endless huge piles of the damn stuff, stretching out into the distance.

It still amazed her, nearly six months after arriving in the Salvage Zone, just how much trash had been dumped out there. Centuries of the stuff, most of it broken machinery, the remains of torn down buildings. A lot of it was rusted metal, dumped there by the civilised world back when there was one. Now that world was long gone and the production of new resources was at a historical low. The Inner Zone officials had decided that it was time to salvage what mankind had scrapped. She'd been told all about the Salvage Zone, and how that entire area of the world had been sectioned off many centuries ago and used as

157

a dumping ground. She had nearly nodded off in the briefing.

She knew that the ark ships, which launched once a year, sending tens of thousands of new resettlers on their fifty year cryo journey to New Earth, needed mountains of metal to construct, and so here she was, overseeing the salvaging operations that made it possible.

Dotted across the landscape were more armoured vehicles, just like the one she now commanded this particular expedition from, and as she watched, one of the vehicles stopped, unloaded its crew of troopers, and then sat waiting for them to return.

Scans, scans and more scans, she thought. The flyby scan had covered an area nearly ten miles across, and had come up with no life signs, but she knew that meant there could still be some. So they had to do it again on the ground, in person, just to make sure. The Junkers were out there somewhere, probably even watching her right now from within their hidden nests, and she had to do whatever was necessary to secure the area before the salvagers arrived.

About a quarter of a mile away, Lisa spotted a vehicle with its hatch still down, even though the troops had been dropped minutes before. She squinted and frowned, wondering why the hatch wasn't shut.

"A3, this is Markel, what is your status? Over."

There was a moment of silence as she waited. And then just as she was about to ask again, a voice replied.

"This is A3. We have a mechanical problem with the door hydraulics. Over."

"Received, A3. Is the rest of the vehicle functional? Over."

"Yes, ma'am. All other functions nominal. Over."

"Okay then, just keep an eye on your entrance, A3. I don't want any unwelcome visitors. As soon as you are all hands on-board, get back to the service truck and get that sorted out. Over."

"Affirmative, ma'am. We have two of the squad in the back of the truck keeping watch. Over."

"Acknowledged, A3. Keep it tight. Out."

Damn inferior machinery, she thought. It had been something she'd noticed in less than a minute of stepping off the Trans into the Recycling Facility. The equipment sent to them from the Inner Zone was almost always the most decrepit, the cast-off trash that had most likely been replaced with something shiny and new. And the vehicles weren't even the same reinforced armoured craft that they used on the Outer Zone raids. No, these things were Inner Zone standard, and would be unlikely to withstand a hit from an automatic weapon without the crew inside being peppered.

Thankfully the only ones with automatic weapons of any kind around here were her people.

Lisa turned to Reece, her second in command, who was standing just a few feet away, staring out at the vast expanse behind them.

"Are we secure?" she asked.

Reece nodded. "Yes, ma'am," he said. "We had some movement a few miles out, which was picked up by the drone, but whatever it was scattered soon after. Thermal scanning hasn't picked anything up."

Lisa nodded and looked back out at the vehicle with the faulty door mechanism. The troopers were back, and getting into the vehicle. A few seconds later the last trooper jumped on board and the door swung clumsily before slamming shut.

"Good," she said. "Let's get the hauler in and clear a staging area. We've got a dozen cans of salvagers due in about four hours and I want this ready."

"Yes, ma'am," said Reece.

"And get that APV with the crappy door booked in with the maintenance crew."

"Yes, ma'am," said Reece.

Lisa turned to head towards the hatch in the middle of the platform, but stopped. "Where are we next, anyway?"

"Ahhh…let me check." Reece took a hand-held touchscreen device from his utility belt, turned it away from the bright glare of the sun, and tapped it a couple of times.

"Facility reclamation mission," he said. "The Picking Factory that was raided by Junkers about ten months ago, over near the blast crater."

Lisa looked relieved. "Nice. We might actually get some activity for once."

JUNK

As far out as you can go.

Jack sneezed as the cloud of dust hit him in the face. He squinted, straining against the bright glare of the sun as he jumped down from the back of the transport vehicle. Even though he was near the back, he was the last one out, after struggling with his safety belt for more than half a minute. As he'd tugged, and tried to reach for the clip, the others filed past and jumped out into the bright sunlight.

Now he found himself standing on dry, dusty ground in a large clearing, maybe two hundred yards across. Where the clearing ended, the flat dry ground finished abruptly at a wall of junk. All around them, piled tens of feet high in some places, was a mass of trash. Most of it was rubble from broken buildings and large sheets of rusty metal, but as his eyes adjusted to the glare of the sun, even from fifty yards away, Jack could see all manner of other things. Rotten wood, decomposing paper and magazines, machinery parts, torn metal structures, and animal bones.

At one section of the junk it looked like whatever

cleared the area – probably a digger of some kind, Jack thought – had torn the trash pile away to reveal an open cavity under a huge pile of trash. Inside the cavity were the rusty remains of an old refrigerator, some smashed up cupboards, and what appeared to be a sleeping cot.

Someone had actually lived there. Hidden right underneath the junk. It must have been a long time ago, had to be. Everything looked so old.

Next to him, the armoured carrier shuddered for a moment and then fell silent as the engines switched off. But the surrounding noise was no less deafening, as no sooner had the vehicle's engine stopped roaring than a second, much larger, vehicle appeared through the roadway carved into the trash. It was a dumper truck, or so Jack thought. It looked like one of the ones used to deliver salvage to the facility, though as it pulled into the middle of the clearing, Jack realised that he had never seen one this close up. The dumpers usually tipped their finds onto the moving platforms outside of the Goods In warehouse, some two hundred yards away from where he worked, and the larger pieces would be sorted and removed before anything even reached the sorting hall.

"Daunting, isn't it?" asked a voice nearby. Jack turned to see Tyler standing just a few feet away. He had tied back his mass of dreadlocks so that they hung down his back through a hole in his jacket, and he'd also pulled a hood over his head. "We have to fill that thing before the end of each day," he said.

Jack looked at the massive dumper, with its huge open — and very empty — back. *You could fit the armoured vehicle that they had travelled in inside, probably twice*, he thought.

"Don't worry," said Tyler, moving to stand next to him. "It'll fill up quicker than you think."

"I don't see how," said Jack.

Tyler laughed and pointed at the back of the armoured carrier. He hadn't noticed the large contraption hooked onto the vehicle's side. "We got a digger," he said. "Boots drives it and drops the heavier stuff in there, while we sift through the crap, looking for the good stuff."

They stood watching Boots and Rick unstrap the one-man digger from the carrier vehicle. As the digger hit the dirt, Jack wondered if Boots would even fit into the thing. It didn't look much bigger than a small car, and it certainly didn't look like it would be able to haul much weight. But Boots squeezed into the tiny compartment at the centre of the digger, and Jack heard some clicking sounds followed by the whirr of a small engine, and the thing sprang to life. *It was compacted for travel*, thought Jack, as the contraption seemed to unfold, changing from a strange upright column into something almost spider-like.

"We'll be out here for about a week," said Tyler. "That's how long we usually stay in one spot before being given a half day out, back at the facility, and then off to the next location."

"A week?" asked Jack. "We stay out here for that long?"

He'd thought that the expedition groups came back every night, but now he thought of the four hour journey to get to this place and realised that there would be no time to work if they spent most of it travelling.

"But where do we sleep?" he asked.

"In the carrier," said Higgins, appearing next to them. He had two rucksacks thrown over his shoulders, and dropped one of them at Jack's feet.

"That's some basic gear for ya," he said. "Mostly left over by Brody…erm… your predecessor."

Jack looked down at the rucksack lying in the dirt.

"Thanks," he said.

"It ain't much," said Higgins. "We could have kept

it all, you know. It's traditional for the dead's gear to get shared out, but we dint need what's in there so you can have it."

"You'll pick up gear along the way," said Tyler. "And anything that the facility don't need that you find out here is your dibs first."

Jack frowned. "We get to keep stuff? I mean, they let us keep things?"

Higgins laughed, almost coughing with the effort. "No, of course they don't let you keep stuff, not if it's useful to them, anyway. But if we don't put it in the back of the dumper, they don't ever knows about it, get it?"

Tyler picked up the rucksack and handed it to Jack.

"What Higgins is saying, is what they don't know about, they don't want. And out here, it's just us."

Jack looked at the digger, and then the carrier.

"But the drivers of the vehicles, surely they see if you take stuff?"

Tyler grinned. "What drivers?"

Jack frowned again.

"Ah," said Tyler. "I get it. Come on," he said. "Come look at this."

Tyler made his way around to the front of the carrier vehicle, and Jack, confused, hurried behind him, trying to fit his new rucksack over his shoulders.

No wonder none of them wants this damn thing. The straps are both ripped.

"There," said Tyler, pointing at the cab of the carrier. "You see the door?"

Jack looked at the side of the cab, and then tried to peer over the top.

"No," he said.

"No, indeed," said Tyler. "That's because there isn't one."

Jack walked around the front of the carrier, peering at the far side, but found it just the same. A sheer metal wall that ended at the front screen. The screen itself was opaque, but Jack had thought they were just designed that way to block visibility of the driver and the rest of the cab crew from the outside.

"It's automated," said Tyler. "They all are." He pointed at the dumper truck. "They can get at them from underneath, to maintain them, but there's no person in there, or even room for one, from what I've heard. It also means no one can steal the damn thing, on account of there being no controls for a human to use."

"You mean that there are no facility staff with us?" asked Jack. "Just us? We're the only ones out here?"

Tyler nodded. "Exactly," he said. "They remote pilot them, or pre-program them, or something. The carrier will remain right there for five days, and then it just goes back, on its own, after the alarm sounds. And it goes with or without us in it. And the dumper goes back every day and comes back before morning, empty."

"Not even guards?"

"Yes, there are guards, but they stay at a central camp about half a mile away from here. That's how they do it. They set up in an area, then they carve out a hole for each of the crews. Now, you see that beacon on top of the carrier? If that starts making one God-almighty noise, you run like hell and get in the back of the carrier, because it seals shut after a couple of minutes whether you're in there or not."

"And what does that mean?"

"It means that something uninvited has moved into our sector."

"Like a creature?"

"Like predators, sure, sometimes. Plenty of those out here, but the radar doesn't look for them and they mostly leave us alone. See, the predators learn faster than people. Usually the siren means that Junkers just got picked up on the radar."

"I see," said Jack. "So, what happens if someone wants to just run off?"

Tyler smiled. "Yeah, sure. We've all thought about it, at one time or another, until we find what's left of someone who did run off."

"Oh. People do, then?"

"Sometimes," said Tyler. "Even had a guy with us about five years ago, ran with us for six months. Before Rick joined us, this guy was part of my crew. Then he decided to make a run for it and took off into the trash. Didn't even bother that we were all watching as he went. Course, he also didn't try to take any gear with him, or we would have stopped him."

"And what happened to him?"

"We found him about three months later, when we cycled back round to the same spot, after Rick had taken his place. Higgins dug him up while we were salvaging. Found him trapped under a pile of crap with both his legs chewed off. He'd got about two hundred yards."

"Damn."

"Oh, yeah. Damn, all right. That wasn't the only

thing eaten. He had no hands and no face. The only way we identified him was his tags. Thought it was a dead Junker until Rick spotted the chain still hanging from his neck. Well, what was left of his neck."

Jack shuddered, and involuntarily reached into his shirt to touch the dog tags that hung there.

"You see, out here," continued Tyler, "you either have the bugs, or you have the Junkers. Both of which will kill you. And no food. Nothing grows out here, it's all lifeless and poisoned. We find bodies every now and then, among the junk. I'm guessing some of them are escapees, but who knows."

Jack nodded, his mind still stuck on an image of a body with no legs sticking out of the junk.

Tyler shrugged. "What I'm saying is, you wanna run for it, no one is going to stop you, but don't expect to take anything with you. We don't waste good gear here."

"I wasn't planning to run," said Jack, but wondered if he really was considering it. Six months was a long time to find no trace of Ryan, and he'd looked everywhere he could at the Facility. Maybe out here, he could search, but where would he even begin?

You have to start somewhere, though. Don't you? But dead isn't a start.

170

"Anyways, as I was saying," said Tyler. "If you hear the siren you run back to the carrier, and don't stop for nothing."

"And then?" asked Jack.

Tyler frowned "Hmm?"

"Then what happens?" asked Jack.

"Nothing. We just wait in the carrier until the drone or the troops arrive to remove the problem. Or until it just goes away."

"What if you're not inside the carrier when they get here?"

Tyler's expression turned from amused to grim.

"Then you become a vacancy."

YOU AGAIN

Lisa Markell wiped the sweat from her face and stared up at the mass of twisted metal in front of her. The huge Drover vehicle had arrived just an hour before, trundling along slowly, as they always did after being left behind to catch up. By the time it had arrived, the salvage groups had already left for their individual areas and the camp had gone into overwatch.

"Can it be repaired in the field?" she asked, looking at the aged mechanic standing just a few feet away, and then at the young trooper standing next to her. Hailey Simmons had been assigned to her expedition just a few weeks before, and Lisa hadn't liked her at first, but the young trooper's can-do attitude soon stopped being irritating, and now Lisa kept her at her side constantly. The girl got things done, or brought things to Lisa's attention much sooner than they otherwise would have been.

Take this drover, Lisa thought. *The driver would have dumped this in the parking ground and walked away, leaving it for what? A day? Two days? Probably three days from now, when I'd want the damn thing hauling along the old roadway and clearing it for us, and we would have been delayed for repairs. Now we get the problem sorted before it's needed.*

"Ah, maybe. Yeah," said the mechanic, rubbing his stubbled chin and looking at the debris jammed into the Drover's cutter. Drovers were originally designed for cutting tunnels in the earth, or even in rock, but they weren't the most robust of contraptions, and when one became no longer of use to the mining sector, they were turned into road clearance trucks, and sent out to make long gouges in the hills and mountains of junk out in the Salvage Zone.

"Maybe?" asked Lisa. "Really?"

"No problem," continued the mechanic, now looking flustered. "I can just cut that out and then we can get in to free the mechanism. Maybe a day?"

Lisa smiled. "Good. Very good. See to it, then. I need this three days from now, to clear a road to an abandoned facility we need to access."

She turned and headed back to the main control centre, a large construction built from a dozen large trucks that could just park next to each other, lower their sides and become one enclosed building. She was relieved to step out of the blistering heat and back into air-conditioned rooms. She headed for the control room, right at the heart of the building, and sat down at her desk.

"Did we manage to re-fill all the group vacancies before we left?" she asked, not even looking round to see if Hailey was with her. Lisa knew she would be.

"Yes, ma'am," said Hailey. "I saw to it myself, as you asked. I picked out some healthy candidates and wrote out the cards last week. It took them a while to process, but we got the replacements just as we were leaving for this trip."

Lisa looked out across the control room, which she always thought was surprisingly large considering it only took up the compartments in three of the trucks. A few yards away was a bank of two dozen LCD monitors, watched by two troopers, all showing different views of the various areas currently being worked by the salvage crews in her expedition group.

"Did you want to review the new replacements?" asked Hailey. "I have them right here."

Lisa was about to say no, but then chuckled quietly. The new recruit was certainly keen to please, she thought, and after how much of a relief she was proving to be, Lisa thought she should at least show interest in the girl's work.

"Sure," she said. "Throw them over here." Then

she turned back to the screens again. The screen at the top right corner was flickering, and that would annoy her very quickly.

Lisa took the thin pile of cards that Hailey handed her. There were a dozen. Had she really lost that many scabs in the last few months? It was hard to tell. There were more than enough accidents out there and, of course, the occasional escapee. It couldn't be helped. But a dozen? That seemed a little high.

She flicked through the cards, checking that the current health status of each individual was marked over ninety out of a possible hundred. *Healthy ones, well done again, Hailey*, she thought.

It wasn't until Lisa flicked to the second-to-last card that she stopped and actually paid some attention to the details. Something had triggered a thought, or a recognition, and it was something on the card before, just as she looked at the last one. Lisa flipped the last card back to the top of the pile and peered at it, curious. What was it about that card that brought back a memory? For a moment she sat there, brow furrowed, just staring at the card, trying to spot what it was about it, or about the individual whose tiny photo stared back at her, that reminded her of something.

The name. Jack Avery. That wasn't familiar, or was it? She'd heard it before. But why was it so important?

Then she recognised the face. It looked cleaner, less pale, and was shaved, but there was the scar above the eyes, just as she remembered.

Well, well. So that's what happened to you, she thought.

"Is everything okay?" asked Hailey.

"Yes," said Lisa. "Fine. Absolutely fine." She handed the cards back to the young recruit. "Good choices, there."

Hailey smiled, and inside Lisa also grinned. The girl was genuinely pleased to be helpful, but that wasn't what made Lisa smile. Jack Avery, the man who had asked who she was, who they were, the man who had given himself up – a thing that no one ever did – and had caused her to remove her visor to speak to him – causing her to be demoted out into this dirty outback – was under her command.

He was one of her salvagers.

I never got answers, Lisa thought. *But now I will have them.*

JUNK

Not alone.

Jack stepped back from the wall of junk and took a deep breath. If it weren't for the hood that he'd managed to fashion the night before from a scrap of dirty cloth that he found in among the trash, he'd have been even hotter. The first day had been fine for about an hour, and then the heat had started to get the better of him.

That was why they all wore hoods, he told himself that evening as he sat in his seat in the back of the carrier, his face and neck red and his head throbbing.

Not one of the other members of the crew had mentioned anything to him, but they were watching him that night as they sat around eating, talking and playing cards on a crate that they hauled out from behind one of the seats.

A rite of passage, maybe? That could be it. That they would put him at risk of heat exhaustion annoyed him a little, but he couldn't deny that these men owed him nothing, and the junk that was in the rucksack – a few spare items of clothing, a utility belt with a bunch of empty pouches on it, a crude knife and fork — they hadn't been obliged to give him them, even if they were what remained of his predecessor's gear.

It didn't matter. He'd fixed it that first night and hadn't said a word to any of them about it, and the following few days had rolled by, hard as the work was, with relative ease. Jack even thought that he caught Tyler smiling to himself when Jack stepped out into the relentless heat the next morning with a hood over his head. It wasn't great, and didn't really keep any of the heat away, but it stopped the sun from burning his already sore scalp.

Now, on the fifth day, after filling the damn dumper truck four times already, he was starting to get past the tiredness that followed in the evening, and even the aches and stiffness in the morning.

And he'd found the entire crew something rare that very morning, only twenty minutes into the start of the day. It was at the back of the caved in dwelling that had been uncovered when they first arrived. That had been the first spot that the crew descended on the minute they started work, obviously spotting the potential that the ancient and abandoned abode could hide, and now, having found the old box behind the wall, he understood why.

He'd followed the rest of the crew over, climbed the

ten or so feet up into the open cavity, and joined them in their search, but Tyler was cursing their luck within a few minutes and claiming that the makeshift home had been abandoned decades ago. Jack had picked up the half-torn and rotten remains of an old magazine that lay in the corner of the dwelling, but the pages were stuck together and most of the paper started to crumble away the second he picked it up.

"The new guy can have this spot," Tyler had mumbled, and Jack had taken his cue from that as the crew left the cavity one by one and took up positions around the clearing.

He'd stood there after they'd left, just looking at the strange cavern that had been carved into the junk, and marvelled at how long the piles of trash had been just sitting there. Centuries. And whoever lived in this dwelling twenty, thirty or even a hundred years ago, had meticulously removed and reinforced the outer walls of the cocoon inside the trash. There was no entrance, and Jack presumed that any way in or out must have been in the section of the hideaway that the diggers had already cleared. Along the walls, scrap metal had been almost woven together and reinforced with plastic covered cables and wires. The floor was constructed from sheets of metal hammered flat – probably car or machine body parts – and then, he presumed, covered in scrap cloth and pieces of carpet. The floor was covered in a mashup of something that must have been cloth or carpet but now, after all this time, it had rotted away into a brown, furry mush.

He moved away, climbing back out of the cavity and down onto the dirt ground below, and looked up at the wall of junk that was now his prospect area.

And he realised he didn't really have much of a clue what he was doing.

I can find stuff, he'd thought. *Sure. I can find value junk inside this mountain of crap, but what am I looking for?* Well, if what got delivered to the sorting area that had had previously worked in was anything to go by, metal and electronics were the thing. So that was where he started, hoping that they didn't send something more valuable that he didn't know about elsewhere.

Two entire days he'd ploughed through the masses of junk, avoiding broken masonry and larger chunks of rubble, relentlessly looking for things made of metal and anything that looked like electronic circuitry. That was their job, it seemed, to crawl among the debris and haul out anything made of metal that could be recycled. It was mindless, and Jack couldn't help but wonder why the hell the city didn't just send out huge automated diggers to haul the stuff away. Surely that would have been more efficient? A half a dozen men, picking away by hand, seemed a slow way to achieve what a digger could do in minutes.

On the third day, Jack had to fling himself away from the edge of the junk as the cavity, and what remained of the uncovered dwelling, collapsed. He'd been picking away at the junk wall in the area surrounding the cavernous hole all that time, pulling bits out, discarding some and keeping others, and gradually the wall had weakened. The cloud of arid dust that spewed out nearly filled the entire clearing, and as he stood up and patted himself down, he heard curses.

But then as the dust began to settle he spotted the box, now newly uncovered where it had been hidden underneath the floor near the back wall of the dwelling for whoever knew how long.

But he'd somehow known it was there. He'd sensed it, like he used to sense lost or concealed things in the ruins of the Outer Zone. He'd felt it from the moment he first saw the dark and open maw of the dwelling. There was something secret in that old place, a precious thing that someone had tucked away and covered over and not wanted anyone to ever find. Even after they were long dead.

He looked around, checking that none of the other crew members had seen it, but the dust still hadn't cleared further across the open ground away from where he stood, and he knew that the nearest to him was Higgins, at least fifty feet away. He hauled the box out from the trash that had compacted underneath the hidden dwelling, looked for a catch of some kind, found it already broken, and slowly, cautiously, lifted the lid.

There was a faint hiss, followed by a musty smell wafting out of the box, and Jack cringed and moved back a short distance, wondering what could make such a stink, but then he peered in, and instead of some nasty, rotten thing in the bottom of the box, Jack spotted a pile of small boxes, each wrapped in a clear plastic jacket and measuring about four inches across.

Cigarettes.

There were twenty packets in all, and they were old, very old.

The box must have been sealed somehow. There was no way that something like that could last that long. How long had it been since cigarettes were made? Hundreds of years? It had to be at least that. He'd heard stories of how, even long after the fall of the old world, a new industrial age had come about in the century before last, and things like cigarettes, canned food, and all manner of more basic goods had started being made again. He'd also heard how that had collapsed because of war. The cigarettes had to have been made then, because for them to come from the old world, well. Did anyone even know how many centuries ago that was? They certainly never came out of the Inner Zone if they were made there. Somehow, he suspected that such things wouldn't be high on the list of things to make for the people inside the barrier-protected city.

And so, that evening, the carrier was filled with smoke, and Jack found himself the lucky owner of a new shirt, a pair of worn but usable gloves, a tin of actual fruit of some kind, a plastic flask that could attach to his utility belt, a tough belt that he could cut up and repair his rucksack with, and even better, a pillow. He guessed that the things were mostly owned by his predecessor, and that it wasn't really much of a loss for the crew members to trade them for a share in the find, but he was happy anyway, sitting there, smoking his first cigarette for months and playing a game of cards.

They'd all heard the noise and fallen silent. Boots was the last to stop laughing, and looked puzzled until he heard the shuffling noises of movement on the ground outside.

Jack frowned, but didn't speak. He looked at Tyler, whose expression had turned serious. Tyler put his finger to his lips to indicate *be quiet*, and then sat there, listening. The inside of the carrier went silent.

There were more crunches of trodden stones from outside the carrier.

Jack looked at Tyler again, and mouthed the words *can it get inside?* But Tyler shook his head.

Jack sat in silence. Listening. Thinking.

Some kind of wildlife. Had to be. But what could live out in this waste? People probably do, though, don't they? Of course they do. Junkers. The ones that they all keep talking about. Mutants. Unclean things. Bugs.

There are a lot of things living out here, you just haven't seen any of them, Jack. That's what Tyler already told you. But they probably wouldn't come near, probably learned from that mistake a long time ago. So what hadn't learned? Something was out there, and whatever that thing was didn't fear the carrier or the people inside it.

There was a banging sound above them, and a thud, thud, as something walked across the roof of the carrier. The sound moved above them, over Jack, then Tyler, then arrived at the top hatch, a thing that Jack had never noticed before. He hadn't even known that there was a top hatch on the carrier.

Another banging sound, and then a groan.

Was that groan made by the thing on the roof? Or was it a noise of something being moved? It sounded metallic, like a rusty box being forced open.

He couldn't know, and decided he didn't want to know.

Then the crunching sound of movement came back, and began to drift away. Whatever it was, it had decided to move on.

It probably wouldn't come back, Jack thought. He hoped it wouldn't. But he didn't sleep very well that night.

UNFORTUNATE

Six Months Before…

An overweight weasel.

That was what the man sitting at the desk in front of Lisa Markell reminded her of. She'd seen pictures in books when she was a kid, dozens and dozens of species of creatures that no one had seen for centuries, presumed extinct, and she remembered the funny picture, and had thought that even the name of the creature was comical. A weasel. And this man looked like an over-fed one at that.

Governor Jackson was, even by standards in the city, an overweight man, and he had a nose that defied gravity. Lisa could never like him. She had decided that the moment the man began to speak to her as she stood across the desk from him, her travel bag still slung over her left shoulder and her assault rifle over the other.

"So you will replace the expedition controller – a Corporal Ranold – who we lost in that…unfortunate incident."

"Why were they all the way out there in the first place?" she'd asked. She hadn't meant to pry, not really, but sending three squads over twenty miles out of the scannable perimeter to the ruins of a town that hadn't been visited for centuries, with little backup, seemed like a frivolous waste to her. Of course, she immediately recognised that Jackson had been the one that made the decision, just by the new flush to his cheeks, and she knew she would regret it, at some point.

"I...err..." stuttered the Governor. "We needed to investigate the area. We're opening up new spots for salvage, and that seemed to be a good place to start."

But you ignored protocol, and failed to make sure that backup teams and supply lines were already in place, she thought, but didn't mention it. She'd already over-stepped.

"But that is irrelevant," continued Jackson, with an irritated glance in her direction. "It was an unfortunate occurrence."

Thirty-six troopers, three entire squads, nine fire-teams, lost. And he considers it unfortunate. No, she would never like him, and was somehow glad that her assignment meant that she would spend the vast majority of her time nowhere near the foul man and his damned facility.

ABANDONED

As she sat in the back of the armoured carrier, just a few hundred yards from the Picking Factory that they were to clear and reclaim, she wondered how many other unfortunate occurrences had happened because of Weasel's orders. It was easy enough for him, sitting there in his air-conditioned building, barely ever having to step outside into the smog and pollution of the world outside, to spend lives. He never had to see the reality of it.

She wondered if the loss of the Picking Factory was something he considered a small loss, something else unfortunate. Two hundred women and children had been there, and yet the place had been guarded by just one squad of troopers. She'd wanted to read that report again, just to remind herself what she was going into, but had thrown it aside in disgust.

Not a single person left behind. That was what the report spelled out. Two hundred women and children, and a single squad of troopers. All taken by the Junkers. It just didn't make any sense to her that they should be out there in the first place, let alone so lightly guarded.

Well, if she saw a Junker today, she was going to make sure that at least that one paid the price.

"Perimeter breach in ten," came the voice of the squad leader in the vehicle at the front of the convoy.

This is it, she thought. *My first actual activity in six months*. She glanced around at the seven other troopers seated in the back of the APV, and her gaze paused when she reached Hailey, now kitted out in combat armour rather than her usual light armour. She imagined that the girl would look nervous if she could see her face, but they were heading into a potentially volatile area and were now wearing full Hunter armour.

It was a necessity, and Lisa was relieved that at least her troopers had that much. From what she had seen of the other supplies and equipment given to the border expeditions, the Hunter armour was a luxury.

Then the back doors were springing open and she was the first out, power-assisted boots hitting the floor and propelling her forward as she skirted around the side of the vehicle and took up position at the very front. The carriers had swerved left upon entering the grounds of the factory, as she had ordered in the briefing earlier that day, and now they were lined up, all four vehicles in a row, just a few yards from the perimeter wall but facing the main building.

Lisa reached to the side of her helmet and switched on her zoom scanner as the rest of her squad swarmed around her to take their positions.

The facility was much larger than she had imagined, even when looking at the rough schematics that she had been sent. Eight large factory hangar buildings rose out of the dirt at least sixty feet high, and they were surrounded by old brick buildings of various sizes, dotted around the outside of the yard.

We could have landed a Dropship inside this place, she thought, looking at the vast open space to the east of the warehouse buildings, but then shrugged that idea off. She knew that the city didn't send Dropships this far out. A thousand miles was much too far for them to send one of those precious flyers, and the fuel alone would make it prohibitive.

She scanned the nearest of the factories, searching for heat signatures and knowing that she would find none. It was nearly impossible, with the distortion of heat from the sun.

No easy way, she thought. *A night raid and we'd see anything lit up like a candle, but with all this debris it would be deadly.*

"Forward," she said into her microphone, and waited.

Five seconds later and the carriers turned and began to slowly crawl across the yard ahead of the Hunter squads. A hundred yards away and they would reach the nearest building, and she would go in there first, herself, leading her team.

And yet she knew, somehow, that this facility would be empty, completely devoid of life. And she also knew that she wouldn't like being the first to discover what had been left behind.

The report said that a scout drone had scanned the facility after the raid. They hadn't even sent a manned operation to go and look. Any unpleasant surprises were still there, waiting for her.

JUNK

Home Sweet Home (Not).

Jack lay on his new bunk in the E2 room trying to get to sleep, but the noise all around him was distracting.

They'd finally finished their five-day stint out in The Junklands, and he couldn't believe how relieved he felt when the carrier halted and the back doors opened up, spilling in sunlight from outside and the familiar waft of dry air.

They were back at the facility.

He had jumped up, hauling his stuff with him, and squinted in the bright sunlight. He'd been five days in the sun, but just a couple of hours in the back of the windowless carrier, with its low light, were enough to make his eyes start to adjust to the darkness.

They had made a good haul, Tyler had said, and he patted Jack on the back as they trudged to their room – to his new room. The tall man was smiling and nodding at Jack now, and Jack took it that he was pleased with his new team member.

Why? Well, after the third day, Jack's unnatural

ability to find what was hidden started to work its way to the surface once more. After discovering the stash under the ruined dwelling, he'd gone on to find several other spots, some not even near his working area, and he uncovered piles of circuitry, some old machinery that looked like it could be rebuilt, and even an old vehicle of some kind, that Jack had never seen before. A tractor, Tyler had said. A whole damn tractor, with the wheels still on it. That thing had nearly filled the dumpster that day, after an hour of Boots struggling with its weight, and after the crew piled a heap of scrap metal into the gaps around the dumpster it was full. All before the sun had even reached its zenith.

And so it went on until the last day. A lot of the time the crew would have to spend hours digging through broken bricks and trash, just to find recyclable metal, but each day Jack managed to cut their working time short by an hour or so, just by knowing where something was hidden.

But now he lay on the bunk, trying to sleep, his head firmly on his new – if somewhat dirty – pillow, and he couldn't drift off. His mind was swirling.

It's not the noise that is distracting, though, is it Jack? It's not knowing where to go next. You hoped to see something out there, didn't you? Something that would lead you back on to the trail of the boy, of Ryan, but all there was out there was endless miles and miles of junk mountains.

And the Junkers. Who were they?

He hadn't seen one of them, but they had visited the carrier twice during the five days. Both times the crew had been tightly secured and tucked up inside the carrier, either playing cards or sleeping, and both times the noise had come from above.

He lay there in the bunk, thinking of Ryan and their last times together, and he watched the crew playing cards in the middle of the room.

During the game, Tyler turned to him. "You don't want to join in?" he asked. "Boots' got a run going here that we can't beat. We need some of your talent here, Lucky Jack."

Lucky Jack. His new nickname, given to him by Higgins after he found the tractor.

"I'm good," he said, meaning a polite no thanks.

Tyler nodded, and turned back again. "We're out to reclaim a facility tomorrow morning," he said. "They took back a Picking Factory that the Junkers stormed a while back, 'bout ten months or so ago, and they want crews up there to shift all the machines out. You reckon you can do some of that magic out there?"

Jack shrugged.

194

"Usually some good stuff left behind by the Junkers if we can get at it first," Tyler continued.

"That the place where all those kids and women got stole from?" asked Higgins. "That old reprocessing and picking plant that was right out in the middle of nowhere?"

Tyler looked at the old man, his expression grim. "I think so," he said.

"That was a nasty thing, right there," said Higgins. "Two hundred women and children, all taken. Poof, just gone, overnight."

Jack wasn't listening right up until the mention of children. Then, he was listening. Listening very carefully.

"Don't, man," said Tyler. "I don't like to think about it."

"What?" asked Higgins. "You don't like the idea of the Junkers taking them, or us going there?"

"Both," said Tyler. "You know they didn't find any bodies, apart from two of the trooper squad, and they were even stripped of all equipment. Shot with their own guns, they reckon, which also means some Junker scum out there now has firearms. I don't know. At least they didn't leave no dead women or kids behind, but it makes me sick wondering what they did do with them."

"Yeah," said Higgins. "Took 'em all, every last one."

Jack sat up. "Took who?" he asked.

The rest of the crew turned to him, and Tyler dropped his cards, the game no longer relevant. "The Junkers raid places occasionally, and I mean in force, like, dozens of them."

"Hundreds, some say," said Higgins.

"Yeah, well," continued Tyler. "About ten or eleven months ago there was a place way out here, a Picking Factory, where they had a couple of hundred kids and some women, and their job was to sort through all the circuitry and small electronics that gets found. You know, the stuff that gets sorted here first. Well, they got sent all the smaller stuff."

Jack thought about how he had spent hours dumping piles of circuit boards, wires, and small broken electronics into large tubs that were then taken away to a truck, and from there to wherever...to the Picking Factory, it seemed. Now there was a very real possibility, if Ryan had gone there, that the boy might have sorted the very stuff that Jack had packed.

"Well," said Tyler. "The Junkers usually only raid and grab supplies, and then run for it, but apparently this time they came in force and took the actual people in the factory, all of them. They don't usually do that. They normally just take stuff and go, often without even having to fight anyone. I mean, if you're faced with a few dozen Junkers charging down on you, most people just up and run like hell and come back when they're gone. This time they took everything they could carry and then some. They took the people, too."

"Apart from a couple of the troopers," said Rick as he lit up yet another cigarette.

"Yeah. Apart from two or three of the trooper squad. They killed them."

Higgins coughed and jabbed at his chest. "You know, that puzzled me," he said. "Junkers eat folks, right? So—"

"There's no proof of that," interrupted Locks. He'd discarded his furry hat on the bunk at the far end of the room, the first time Jack had seen him without it perched on his head even when sleeping, and Jack could see that he had a large round bald spot on the top of his head. "No one actually got proof that they eat people, and no one has seen them doing it. Anyone found eaten out in the junk could easily have been got at by one of the bugs."

"Oh but that's what everybody says," said Higgins. "Everyone knows Junkers eat anything, including each other."

"That's what people say," said Locks. "And they also say that some of those bugs out there can talk, but that's absolute rubbish, yeah?"

Higgins shrugged. "Well, maybe. Whatever. But that's what I'm saying. If they do eat people, then why dint they take the bodies of the troopers? Or just cook 'em right there?"

"I don't know, okay?" interrupted Tyler. "And I don't even want to think about it. And anyway, we get to see first-hand what they left behind, because we're on clean up and reclaim duty, as of tomorrow."

That was why Jack couldn't sleep. The Picking Factory, a place that used to have hundreds of kids working in it, seemed to be the very first sign of any significance that might lead him to Ryan's trail. If there was a place that the boy could have ended up, it had to be there. Jack had found nowhere else, no other leads.

But the Junkers had raided the place, and that meant another possibility that Jack didn't want to consider. But he found it too hard not to dwell on it.

WAITING FOR TIME

Lisa sat on top of the armoured truck and watched as the convoy of salvage carriers trundled noisily into the yard of the Picking Factory. They were two hours late, and she had been pacing back and forth for most of that time before finally settling on just sitting and waiting. It was pointless calling anyone, and it didn't matter what the delay was. They would get there when they got there.

The last truck, the one with the big grey letters E2 painted on the side, was the one she was most interested in. He would be in that one, that much she knew. She hadn't gone over to the salvagers' bunk rooms – no, that would have seemed strange. If she'd turned up there just to find Jack Avery, everyone would be talking about it. So she had been patient but made sure that the E2 crew was assigned to this duty, and now she waited.

Next to her, also looking relieved to see the crews arrive, Hailey was busy scribbling on her clipboard.

"Why don't you use a touch pad?" Lisa asked.

Hailey looked up from her scribbling and frowned. "I don't have one," she said.

"Oh," said Lisa. "I'll fix that."

Hailey nodded. "Two hours fifteen behind schedule, but at least they're all here," she said.

Trust Hailey to find a bright spot among the gloom, thought Lisa. She stood up, pushing away from the armoured wall that surrounded the flat platform on top of her command vehicle.

"And we're two hours plus behind," she said. "They better have a good reason for it."

Hailey looked up once more. "I'll find out why," she said.

JUNK

The Past Comes Back.

The officer was watching him, Jack was convinced. It was difficult to tell for sure. The helmet, similar to those worn by the Hunter troops in the ruins of the Outer Zone but more worn and damaged, hid the face behind it, but that blackened and domed visor was pointing in his direction and he could almost feel the gaze upon him as he bundled his gear out of the back of the carrier and threw it over his shoulders.

The scabs stood in an inspection line with Tyler at the front. This had not been mentioned to Jack, but he just fell in line with the rest of them as the crews assembled in the yard next to their vehicles. The troop officer, and another trooper that Jack presumed was a junior officer, walked along the line and then moved away.

That officer definitely stopped at him for longer than the others, he thought, and noticed even Tyler was frowning at him. Curiosity, no doubt. If Tyler had noticed it as well then it wasn't just his imagination.

But the officer said nothing to him, just stared at

him for a few seconds and then moved on. Then Tyler and the other crew leaders were called aside, moving across the dusty yard to stand with the officer. They were speaking, but what about?

He couldn't hear the conversation, so instead looked away and stood there, taking in his surroundings.

The facility was huge, much larger than he had expected. Though he hadn't known what to expect, really. The word factory made him think of the coal yard, back when he had been a kid. That had to be it. He'd expected a single crumbling building with a yard and a perimeter fence, but of course this was quite far away from the Recycling Facility, and isolated.

Why would they send so many people so far out? This was Badlands, and uncontrolled. Anything could be — and was — scurrying around out here. Junkers, whatever they were — people of some kind? And bugs. He'd seen neither, but the men on his crew had told him that they were both something to be feared.

"Like some kind of screwed up mutant," Higgins had said, when asked about the Junkers. "They might have been human once, but they were like, part-machine, part-animal or something. I saw it from a distance, just before the siren went off, standing right up on top of the junk and looking down on me. It had this thing, a weapon, like some kind of spear but with a nasty blade on the end. I ran for it. Something about that thing. It wanted to eat me, I'm sure of it, and the hell it wasn't afraid of the carrier or me."

It seemed hard to imagine that a human could degenerate into something entirely different, Jack thought, but then, he'd seen the Night Ones in the Outer Zone, even if from a distance, and they seemed far from human.

Maybe that was what the Junkers were like? The Night Ones. He tried to remember the time he and Drogan had been caught out in the ruins near the Ashlands. The night they had been chased. The last time he'd ever seen his friend.

JUST RUN

Many Years Before.

The camp-fire was roaring. Drogan had seen to that. Out in the reaches near the Ashlands the air was bitter cold all year long, even when other places were baking with the summer sun. Jack had never liked going that far out, but his friend insisted on it when things were tight and they had found no salvage to trade for a few weeks.

And this was one of those times. They'd searched further and further out in the last few weeks, after heading east from The Crossing, and they'd even gone into areas that neither of them had travelled before, but the picking had been getting harder and harder.

That was the one good thing about the borders near the Ashlands. There was still plenty to be found, for those willing to risk going anywhere near the creatures that lived in the ash wastes. And if you lit a good fire, bright and hot, those things left you well alone anyway.

He'd always wondered why that was. The Night Ones, as many folks called them, were humanoid but far from being living people. Jack suspected that once, centuries ago, they may well have been people, but the pale skinned and rotten creatures that screamed and howled in the frozen ash wastes were nothing like people now.

Until that night, while the fire roared and Drogan cooked the two skinny rabbits that they'd caught a few hours before, Jack had only seen them from a distance.

But the wind was stronger than usual, gusting in across the crumbling ruins and blowing so hard that he'd nearly toppled over several times.

Then, later, when the darkness of night came and the screaming and howling began to resound from across the ash wastes, one almighty gust of wind blew through the broken remnants of the building they had taken refuge in and the fire just went out.

And the next few minutes were the most terrifying of his life.

He heard, more than saw, Drogan hurrying to relight the fire, and Jack scrambled toward the noise and tried to help. But it was no good. The wood that they had found was wet on the inside, and only the outer layers had took light. Now they just couldn't seem to get the thing to catch again, even when Jack used his body to block the wind, hoping that Drogan could at least get something going.

But Drogan stopped.

"We have to get the hell out of here," he said, and in the moonlight, Jack's vision now adjusting to the lower light that only the moon provided, he could see real fear in the man's eyes. They had travelled for nearly four years together, side by side, scavenging in the ruins and trading at the hovels, and Jack had never once seen Drogan look frightened, even when they had had to face down a gang of rovers three times their number.

But now the moonlight showed Jack a face full of fear.

They scrambled around the camp, grabbing their gear and stuffing it in packs, and a minute later were jogging alongside each other, away from the already chilling campfire.

"This was stupid," Drogan had said. "I should never have brought us out here."

"It was only the fire," Jack had replied. "If that hadn't gone out we'd have been fine."

Drogan didn't rely. He just continued to trudge alongside Jack.

"And anyway," continued Jack. "We found a tonne of stuff to trade, and we can just go further into the ruins for a couple of miles, find a place with higher walls, and make another camp."

"I suppose," said Drogan. "But I still think that—"

There had been a flash of movement from their right that zipped past Jack and slammed into Drogan. The man cried out and went down hard, struggling to his feet a couple of seconds later.

Jack already had his machetes out and stood there, on the spot, next to his friend, turning left and right, scanning the darkness for more movement.

"The hell," cursed Drogan, finally getting to his feet.

"What was that?" asked Jack.

Drogan shook his head. "I don't know," he said. "But let's not hang around to find out, eh?"

And so they had continued on, moving faster now.

And it was a few minutes later, just as they began to spot the outlines of larger ruins in the distance, the walls faintly lit by the moon, that the scream resounded from just a few feet away.

"Run," shouted Drogan, taking off at full pelt in front of Jack, and Jack had followed, urging himself onwards as fast as his feet could carry him, his lungs screaming for air and his muscles protesting at every lunge forward.

Jack caught up with Drogan and passed him, but not by much. He didn't want to push on, didn't want to split up with his friend. But then, as he ran onwards, he felt, more than saw, movement all around them. There were no more screams, but the gaunt figures that loped alongside them at a distance were not silent anymore. Growls and hisses assaulted his ears.

And then there was another flash of movement next to them, and Drogan vanished with a startled cry, going down onto the hard road with a slam that Jack heard. And he also heard something crack.

Drogan cried out once more, and then the cry turned into a scream.

Jack turned back, swinging his machetes at the darkness around him, but nothing came near him. There was a mass of movement ahead of him, right where Drogan had gone down, but Jack was struggling to make out what it was.

Figures. Dozens of them, crawling all over each other and pushing, shoving, trying to get to Drogan.

"Run, you idio—" came the last thing Jack would ever hear his friend say, the words cut off as a gargling, bubbling rasp replaced them.

But Jack had hesitated for a moment, not wanting to leave his friend to die. Whatever those things were, the Night Ones, surely he could fight them.

He ran at the mass of bodies, hacking at anything

that moved, until a few remaining creatures ran from him, leaving a dozen or more of their kin lying dead. He'd seen red for that few seconds and stormed into the creatures with a rage that he didn't know he had. Life, death — none of it mattered. Drogan was in trouble.

And then Jack was panting, his chest heaving with exertion as he tried to breathe, but Drogan was on the ground in front of him, and Jack could see there was nothing at all that he could do to help his friend.

So he'd turned and run that night, not even stopping to pick up any of the gear that had once been his friend's.

Someone else could have that if they dared.

Someone else could find Drogan's equipment if they really wanted to face the creatures out in the Ashlands. Because Jack vowed that he would never return.

JUNK

No. The Junkers couldn't be like the Night Ones, Jack thought. He hoped. They couldn't be. Night Ones would never have known how to use a weapon to kill the troopers left behind at the Picking Factory. The things he'd seen that night were no more human than a rabid rat. They had been things twisted beyond recognition, dead but not dead, pale skinned and gaunt, their eyes hollow black pits that were lifeless.

And if there were Night Ones out here in The Junklands, then the people running the Recycling Facility surely wouldn't have left so many people out here unguarded.

But that doesn't answer your question, does it?

Why had they left all those kids and women out here? It didn't make much sense to him. It was almost like asking for them to be taken. It had to be…what? Five hours from the main facility. And from what he had heard from Tyler and the others, they had only manned this place with a single detachment of troopers.

And the bugs? Nasty long-legged things that darted over the junk like it was a flat path, and very fast, or crawling beetle-like things, hidden away deep inside the piles of debris, nesting and waiting to be uncovered. That's how Higgins had described them, and Jack hoped never to meet either of those.

All these things went through his mind as he stood there in the blazing sun, looking out across the massive facility that they now had to clear. Rows of huge monolithic buildings lined the centre of the vast, dry, open space, and beyond that, where the perimeter wall stood crumbling, with huge gaps collapsed to the ground, smaller buildings stood.

There has to be a hundred buildings here. How are you possibly going to find any trace of Ryan? Had he been out here when the place was attacked? It sounds likely, doesn't it? This is the place to start looking, after six months of finding nothing in the Recycling Facility. A place to start.

But what if you do find something? What then?

"Okay, listen up," came the deep boom of Tyler's voice, drawing him from his daze and snapping him back into the present. "We got dealt the far compound, where the big machines are, and after that we have the living quarters and the outer buildings on the far side. That's us for the next five days." Tyler squinted in the bright sun and scratched his chin. "Usual drill, though we're being told that the carrier will be moving over there." He turned and pointed at the large open space

211

between the huge central buildings and what looked to be some kind of hangar.

"Five days here?" snapped Higgins. "That long just to clear out a few machines?"

Tyler shrugged. "What do you know?" he said. "I guess there's more here than I expected. More than just a couple of machines, anyway. Maybe we'll find something sweet in all the rot? Never know. Let's get back on board and wait."

They headed back over to the carrier and Jack stood at the end of the line, waiting to climb on-board. Higgins was muttering something to himself about wasting time, but Jack didn't catch all of it. He was too busy looking past the crew, over to where the officer and the other troopers were standing.

The officer was watching him again.

YOU AGAIN

It was definitely him, Lisa thought. He was less scruffy than he'd been when he gave himself up, speaking to her that day at the back of the armoured carrier in the middle of the Outer Zone ruins. But she recognised him instantly. He was tall, though not as tall as some of her men, and he was built well. Strong, even though most of the prisoners were underfed.

Now she had found him again, she was unsure of what difference it made. She'd hoped for something, whatever it might be, when she caught up with him again, but she didn't know what. And it wasn't like she could just initiate a conversation with him, ask him the questions that were bugging her. It wasn't the done thing.

I have to just watch and wait, she thought. *Watch and wait for the right moment.*

The man probably didn't even know it was me, that I'm the same one he surrendered to. Lifting her visor would have solved that, but she remembered that doing just that was exactly what had landed her this wonderful job out in The Junklands in the first place.

And what about that? She thought that she would

be angry with the man when she finally met him again, thought that she would blame him for everything that had happened to her since then. Why had she shown her face in the first place? Why make any form of contact? It didn't make sense, not to her, anyway.

And now, having met him again, she didn't feel angry at all. The guy was in a much worse situation than she was. She'd sleep in an air-conditioned armoured transport with a bunk tonight, and he would be bunked down with a bunch of stinking scabs.

He won't have found his boy, either, will he? She thought. *All this time, and he has probably found nothing. There were no kids at the main Facility, they never took them there. Most of the ones that came out here were sent to the Picking Factories, like the one they stood in right now.*

Had the boy been here?

Damn it, she cursed silently. Why the hell should she care about a boy she'd never met? There were hundreds here when the raid happened, she knew that much. Hundreds taken by the Junkers. And what had happened to them? Dead? Were they killers, these things that lived out in the waste? They'd killed troopers – that much she knew – but children and women? Were those things even human enough to know the difference?

214

It annoyed her immensely every time she thought about it. Governor Jackson had sent them all out here with just one squad of security, just twelve troopers, and they had been taken, captured by the Junkers. The troopers were either killed or also taken, and that foul creature, Jackson, shrugged it off as unfortunate.

No, he didn't actually say this incident was unfortunate, she thought. That had been the disappearance of three squads, months before. But she could bet that it would be his reply if she'd asked.

Maybe I can find some clues out here, she thought. *Maybe those people are retrievable.*

That would be an achievement.

JUNK

The Past Comes Back.

He found it on the second floor of the last workshop and just stood there, staring at it.

Three days ago they had entered the first warehouse. As Tyler had said, E2 crew was to do the last three warehouses and then all of the outbuildings on the north side of the facility, and that included a number of workshops and smaller factory buildings as well as the area that had been used as a dormitory.

They'd entered the first warehouse, Jack at the back of the crew, carrying a heavy shoulder-load of cutters and some matt sheeting. Tyler was up front with Higgins next to him, the other men following. They'd all stood there for a few minutes, gazing around the massive interior of the dilapidated old building, just looking, in awe of the massive installation that they were apparently supposed to take apart.

The floor was flat concrete and, apart from a few crumbling bits of masonry in the corners, was well swept and barely cracked. The ground was worn and looked like it had been well trodden over the years, and in some spots the bare ground even appeared smooth. If there had been doors on the building then there was no evidence of them now. Huge open spaces, looking out onto the dusty ground outside, let the sun blaze into the interior, and Jack had been surprised that the ground wasn't covered in sand and dirt from outside. But somehow it wasn't.

And the sprawling array that was the picking plant sat smack in the middle of the wide-open space. Large hoppers lined one wall, with belt-fed conveyors coming out of the bottom and leading across the open ground, splitting in several places before passing raised platforms that lined long stretches of belt.

Where the kids would have stood and sorted stuff, Jack thought.

The raised platforms were rusted and cracked, and behind them, stacked up high, were metal bins with wheels on the bottom. Mini dumping trucks for whatever the kids must have been taking off the conveyors lines.

He stood there, the dry wind buffeting his back and the heat of the sun burning his bare arms, and imagined what the place had been like when it was active, when it was busy with dozens of children sorting through the crap that must have been sent there. In his mind, the conveyors were moving, making a *clunk clunk* noise as each section bumped over the supporting joists. And he imagined a row of young children, from the very small right up to teenage years, lined along the platforms, poking around in the junk that passed and throwing what they found into the metals bins behind them.

He saw other children, two at a time, pushing the metal bins away to one corner of the warehouse and then pushing another empty into its place.

They were dirty kids, filthy and covered in the grime that rubbed off onto their hands from the junk passing along the conveyors, and their faces were smeared with dust and sand that blew in from the outside.

"Well, we better get started," said Tyler.

Jack looked up, snapping out of his daydream and saw the tall man had turned and was looking back at his crew. "We got to take all this down, cut it up and get it hauled out to the dumper."

"Dumper isn't even here yet," said Rick, coughing into his hand and then wiping it on his shirt.

"No," said Tyler. "But we may as well get on the go anyway."

Jack spent most of the three days, until they moved into the workshops along the north side, cutting up the conveyors' parts and snipping down the sides of the bins, stacking them up near the main entranceway when the dumpster truck wasn't there. By the time they left the three warehouses, and moved into the workshops, his hands were sore, even through his gloves.

On the third day they moved out of the warehouses and started with the outbuildings, and he was relieved. The heat inside the warehouses was almost unbearable, and the temperature dropped significantly when they entered the smaller, stone-built buildings.

And so it was that, just an hour before the sun went down and they would be due to head back to the carrier and rest up for the night, he climbed the six flights of stairs to the top floor of the workshop that they were emptying.

The building was filled with work benches, lines and lines of them in every room, and on each bench was a mess of mechanical and electronics parts. Wound up spools of wires, cutting tools, knives, snippers, hammers, all manner of tools – a lot of which he knew would never make it into the dumpster and would instead be hidden away inside the personal bags of many of his crew. There was just too much treasure lying around all over the place for it not to.

They'd cleared the bottom floor, moved up to the second, and the rest of the guys, led by Higgins, were busy hauling the contents down to the ground floor with ropes and buckets.

"Why don't you go check-up top?" Tyler had suggested. "Give us a scoop on what's up on the last floor, ready for tomorrow. Then come down to bottom and grab a smoke."

Jack had nodded. "No problem," he'd said.

And so he headed up the stairs and onto the raised gantry that led along all of the north side buildings. It looked like an outer defence platform that spanned most of the north side of the facility, with metal stairwells in between the buildings. He wondered for a moment if they would need to take that down as well. It was, after all, made of metal, and that was the resource most wanted by the Recycling Facility. Metal and electronics.

He shrugged and stepped out of the bright sun and into the huge open interior of the top floor and looked straight at it.

There was an old stairwell at the side of the big room, though it had long since crumbled and collapsed. Inside the stairwell the floor opened up into a drop that went all the way down to the bottom floor, but that wasn't what Jack saw.

I NEED ANSWERS

Lisa watched as the man fell to his knees, but she didn't rush forward to help him. Instead she stood there, watching, as she had the whole time.

He hadn't noticed her as he had come up the stairs and out onto the gantry, and she hadn't expected him to. She was a hundred yards away, near the next building, watching out over the sprawling landscape of junk that began fifty feet from the outer wall, and she was tucked inside an alcove away from the heat of the sun.

Her combat armour protected her from the rigours of the hot sun, from most weather in fact, but only if she was fully suited. And she hadn't wanted to be at that moment. Sitting up there on the gantry, watching out for movement far away, she preferred to take her helmet off.

And so she'd seen him enter the workshop and realised he was alone.

She glanced down and counted the crew members on the ground in the yard below. It was a full crew except for him. No one else up there. He was alone.

WHAT JACK SAW

There was some flooring inside the stairwell. Pieces of wood that had probably once been the top of the stairs jutted out from the wall like broken and rotten teeth. Just far out enough, he thought, for someone to step round if they didn't weigh too much. He would have collapsed them with his weight, but a boy, maybe one only six, seven, or eight years old, and thin, would have been able to walk around them like a ledge to the small platform at the back that would have been the eave over the stairs, a spot most likely unnoticed by most people.

But this also wasn't really what Jack had noticed. That was all small, peripheral detail that flooded in as he stared at the top wall over the hole that would have been the stairs. The wall was a pale colour, and he thought that it was coated in paint that somehow still remained after so many years. It was, after all, tucked away inside a building and away from the wind. And it was a light-coloured paint, cracked and dry near the corners and edges of the wall, but the paint covering most of the flat surface was still smooth and clear, even if it was somewhat stained.

Covering most of the surface of the wall were drawings. He didn't know what they had been drawn with, maybe a piece of charcoal, or something else dark in colour. Even a charred piece of wood could have been used. The figures were all stick-men, and they were busy little stick-men. Two of them were sitting on a step of some kind with bowls in their hands.

Eating ant soup, he thought.

Another two stick-men were rifling through a pile of trash, and the smallest of the stick-men was throwing bits over its head.

Scavenging in the ruins.

And then there were another two, walking and pushing a cart of some kind, the smallest riding on the front of the cart and the larger one pushing with its back hunched over.

Off to The Crossing to sell the finds.

And there, smack in the middle of the dozens of similar, tiny scenes that were scrawled all over the wall, were the same two stick people.

One tall and one small, standing holding hands.

And that was when Jack's knees went from under him.

Finally, he thought. *Finally, I found where you went.*

CONTINUED IN BOOK TWO...

BOOKS BY GLYNN JAMES

ALTERLIGHT Book 1 "Where the lost go"
ALTERLIGHT Book 2 "The Calling of Wolves"
ALTERLIGHT Book 3 "In Chasing Spirits"
THROWN AWAY Book 1 "In a Fallen World"
THROWN AWAY Book 2 "What Lies Below"
THROWN AWAY Book 3 "Another Man's Gold"
THROWN AWAY Book 4 "Return"
THROWN AWAY Book 5 "To Ashes"
DIARY OF THE DISPLACED Book 1 "The Journal of James Halldon"
DIARY OF THE DISPLACED Book 2 "The Broken Lands"
DIARY OF THE DISPLACED Book 3 "The Ways"
DIARY OF THE DISPLACED Book 4 "Footprints"
DIARY OF THE DISPLACED Book 5 "Where no River Falls"
DIARY OF THE DISPLACED Book 6 "Redux"
ARISEN Book 1 "Fortress Britain"
ARISEN Book 2 "Mogadishu of the Dead"
ARISEN Book 3 "Three Parts Dead"
ARISEN Book 4 "Maximum Violence"
ARISEN Book 5 "Exodus"
ARISEN Book 6 "The Horizon"
ARISEN Book 7 "Death of Empires"
ARISEN Book 8 "Empire of the Dead"
DUSTFALL Book 1 "Shadows of a Lost Age"
DUSTFALL Book 2 "The Parting of Ways"
DUSTFALL Book 3 "The Baying of Wolves"
DUSTFALL Book 4 "Sons of the Lost"
DUSTFALL Book 5 "What Lies beneath"

ABOUT THE AUTHOR

GLYNN JAMES is an author of science fiction, post-apocalyptic, dark fantasy, horror, and dystopian fiction. His love of science fiction began when he was eight years old after discovering HP Lovecraft and Richard Matheson, and then later on Terry Pratchett, Neil Gaiman, James Herbert, Clive Barker, and Stephen King.

In addition to being author of the "ALTERLIGHT" supernatural mystery thriller series, he is author of the dark sci-fi series "DIARY OF THE DISPLACED", the post-apocalyptic "THROWN AWAY" series, and co-author of the "ARISEN" series and the "DUSTFALL" series.

More info on his writing and projects can be found at -

Website - www.glynnjames.co.uk

Facebook –

https://www.facebook.com/glynnjamesfiction

Goodreads - https://www.goodreads.com/GlynnJames

COPYRIGHT

First published 2021 by Glynn James

Printed in Great Britain
by Amazon